CRY OF THE WOLF

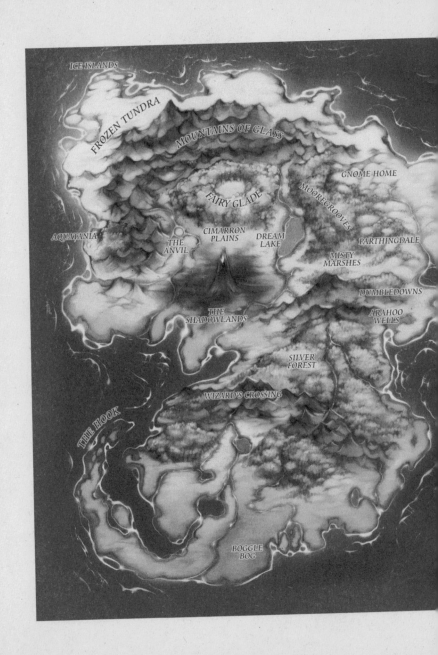

LOST MOUNTAINS

SALT SEA

FIRE
DESERT

SECRET FOREST

CRYSTAL PEAKS

PORT
BERRY

SNAKE
RIVER

SOUTHERN
PLAINS

TWILIGHT JUNGLE

PORT TUGA

PIRATE'S
COVE

GIANT'S FOOTPATH

ALDENMOR

N

1

SUNLIGHT FLASHED THROUGH the trees as the dark-haired girl ran, plunging wildly into the woods. Yellow, orange, and red leaves crunched under her boots as she dashed past towering maples, cherries, and ash. It had recently rained, and the woods smelled clean and crisp.

"Follow my voice."

Adriane Charday heard the words in her mind as clearly as if they had been spoken aloud. Listening closely, she turned toward an outcropping of rocks and leaped over a downed log, running hard, breathing steadily.

"You're getting cold."

Adriane turned sharply left, her long, jet-black hair blowing in her face. "We'll see about that."

With a quick sweep of her wrist, she cut her gemstone through the air. It sparkled gold from its setting in her black-and-turquoise bracelet, and Adriane smiled, confident she was on the right trail.

It had been a month since she and Emily and Kara had learned about the magic web: the network of magical energy that connected Earth to other worlds. They had discovered a portal to a world called Aldenmor and learned of the Dark Sorceress, her attempts to capture magical animals, and of the horrible Black Fire poison. At first, both monsters and animals from Aldenmor had come through the portal—right into the Ravenswood Wildlife Preserve, where Adriane lived with her grandmother. The animals all spoke of Ravenswood as a legendary sanctuary of magic and it had to be protected. With the help of some pesky little creatures called dragonflies, the three girls had woven a magical dreamcatcher over the portal, hoping it would let good things through while keeping evil creatures out.

But with magic you just never knew. The dragonflies didn't seem to need a portal at all—they just popped in and out of nowhere. Banshees that had stalked Kara had been able to move through water, and had even attacked her in the Jacuzzi. One thing was sure: magic was unpredictable. They had to expect the unexpected.

The discovery that magic was real was the most

monumental thing that had ever happened to the girls. What was even more astounding was that each of them seemed to have a part to play in a larger puzzle, a mysterious destiny that required each girl's own unique talents as mages, human users of magic. Elemental beings were trying to protect the good magic of Aldenmor. They were called Fairimentals and according to some ancient prophecy they needed a healer, a warrior, and a blazing star to do . . . something. What that something was exactly, the girls didn't know. Neither did their magical animal friends. But whatever it was, it involved finding a mysterious hidden place, the home of all magic: Avalon.

Emily, the healer, spent a lot of time with the magical animals that had made Ravenswood their new home. When she wasn't with them or helping out at the Pet Palace, she was in Ravenswood Manor's incredible library, cataloging information about wildlife, both earthly and magical. More and more, too, she had emails to answer, as curious people began to surf their way to the Ravenswood blogs the girls had set up.

Kara, the blazing star, was President of the Ravenswood Preservation Society. She spent half her time setting up tour schedules, planning fund-raising parties, and reporting on their progress to her father, the mayor. The other half she spent making sure the town council never found out about the magical animals hidden at Ravenswood. Not all the members of the town council wanted a wildlife tourist attraction outside of their town, and Kara had to keep them reassured about their decision to keep the preserve open with the girls working there as guides.

Adriane felt it was essential to learn all she could about the magic she shared with her wolf friend. Her name was Stormbringer and she was a mistwolf, a creature of great magic. Storm had called Adriane "warrior" from the first moment they had met and the girl spent every spare moment practicing, experimenting, pushing herself further and faster, obsessed with embracing her new abilities, scared she could lose them.

She took a deep breath of crisp autumn air and lengthened her strides, stretching into the run. She and Storm had been playing this new game of hide-and-seek for about two weeks now, experimenting with the magic of her tiger's eye gem called the wolf stone. Each time Storm moved farther away, testing the limits of their connection. How far could they go from each other before the connection was lost? So far, they hadn't reached the limit—if there was one.

Through the trees, Adriane caught a trail of mist vanishing over a rise. She made a sharp right, and then sprinted up the hill, trying not to slip on the moss.

Brow furrowed, she concentrated on her stone and was rewarded with a quick image in her mind of Storm. The big silver-and-white wolf was just on the other side. With a grin, she crested the top, and leaped.

"Adriane!" Storm's voice cut through her mind. *"Watch out for that—"*

The image of the wolf vanished as Adriane flew through trails of fog with a startled cry.

"Oof!"

Her shoulder knocked into something hard and she landed in a pile of sticky leaves and twigs. Facedown.

Storm was loping toward her, tongue lolling.

"—tree," she finished.

The tree's oversized leaves had been holding rainwater—until Adriane had bumped into it. She glared up through her now sopping-wet bangs. "Thanks for the heads up."

"Are you all right?"

"I was concentrating so hard on seeing you, I didn't see what was right in front of me."

The wolf seemed to be laughing. *"You must learn to see the tree through the forest."*

Adriane spit out a piece of leaf. "That's forest for the trees." She sat up, picking matted leaves from her face and hair. "Oh, look at me!"

"Wait a minute," Storm commented. *"I think you missed a spot."* Her tongue flashed out, licking a bit of leftover leaf from Adriane's chin.

"Cut it out!"

The wolf's golden eyes danced with mischief. *"Hold it. Here's another one."*

Adriane squealed as Storm planted her big paws on

the girl's chest, knocking her flat onto her back, her tongue slobbering over every inch of her face.

"Forget it, that doesn't help!"

Storm lowered her head and pulled back.

Giggling, Adriane dug her fingers into the thick fur at the wolf's neck, then gave a heave and flopped her over. Together, girl and wolf rolled across the hill, then lay still, side by side, panting.

Adriane's down vest was now covered in leaves. Storm's coat had twigs sticking out of it.

"You look ridiculous," Adriane said, giving the wolf's stomach a thump.

"A mistwolf never looks ridiculous," Storm informed her. She rolled over onto her back and stuck her legs in the air, twisting from side to side in an attempt to dislodge the debris from her coat. *"Mistwolves are dignified and fierce."*

And alone, Adriane thought suddenly, her smile fading. There were no other mistwolves. Storm was the last of her kind.

Was it fate, or destiny, or just some haphazard random coincidence that she had met Storm? Maybe she'd just been lucky.

She sat and gazed at the forest spread out below. The autumn colors rippled like wildfire, blazing under the noon sun. Storm sat down beside her. Draping an arm over the wolf's back, Adriane pointed to a clearing in the forest off to the west. "See there by the Rivanna

River?" she asked. "That field is where I first found my stone, and you."

She looked at the beautiful amber-and-gold stone, the same color as the oak leaves that gently spiraled around them. She didn't know where the stone had come from; she knew only that finding it had made her feel special, as if it had been put there just for her. In her hands, the rough stone had transformed into a smooth, polished jewel in the shape of a wolf's paw, and a bond was made, forged like iron between a lone wolf and a lonely girl.

Taking a deep breath of crisp fall air, she leaned against Storm, comforted by the solid strength and furry warmth of the wolf. It occurred to her that just as the mistwolf's solid form could evaporate into mist, so could this luck disappear. Wasn't that what always happened? She felt the familiar knot of fear in her stomach starting to build.

Adriane remembered when she first arrived at Ravenswood, not even a whole year ago. She hadn't wanted to live with her strange grandmother in a weird house. She didn't want to have anything to do with Stonehill, Pennsylvania, at all.

This is *not* my home, Adriane had thought. And no one can make me say it is!

She'd been all over the world and had lived in all kinds of places because her parents were famous artists. Some people might think that was glamorous. It wasn't. It was lonely. Always moving from place to place. Never feeling she belonged.

She frowned. They hadn't even come with her—they had just dropped her off with a grandmother she barely knew and flew off again to who-knew-where. They sent postcards . . . sometimes.

"Do you want to talk about it?" the wolf asked.

Adriane made a face. "No."

"That probably means you should."

"What are you, my counselor or something?"

Storm didn't answer, and Adriane continued to lean against her, listening to the wolf's heartbeat, feeling the way Storm's chest moved in and out with each breath.

"My parents stuck me here, and I won't even see them till next summer," she said quietly into the wolf's soft fur. "They don't want me." There it was—she'd finally said the thing that had been a hard, hot ball of pain ever since she'd come to Stonehill.

Her parents didn't want her.

Like Storm, she was alone.

"You're feeling sorry for yourself again, aren't you?" Storm asked. *"You get this funny look on your face."*

"I do not." Adriane sat up.

Her long, dark hair fell over a scowling face. She knew she was acting like a grumpy two-year-old, gearing up to throw a tantrum. She tried to calm herself. "How come my closest friend in the world has four feet?"

Storm gave a strange bark that Adriane recognized as wolfish laughter. *"You're just incredibly lucky."*

Adriane grinned. "Did I miss out on the 'plays well with other humans' gene or something?"

Storm touched her cool nose to Adriane's cheek. *"I was without a pack until I met you."*

"What happened to the mistwolves, Storm?"

"They vanished. I have some memories from Aldenmor, but I feel like I have always been here, connected to the forests of Ravenswood."

"Don't you want to find out?"

"Our paths have led to each other. And together we will find the answers we seek."

"I can't even find you without a magic stone."

"You are my packmate. You will always find me."

"How can I be sure?"

Storm's warm golden eyes turned to look into Adriane's dark ones. *"Our bond is sure. Hold it tight and never let go."*

"I won't, Storm. Not ever." She hugged the wolf, burying her face in the soft silver fur. "It's everything."

"You must trust in your gifts."

"Sometimes you sound just like a human grown-up," Adriane said.

"There's no need to be insulting," Storm replied.

Adriane snorted. Storm had been right, as usual. Talking about the things that bothered her always helped, even if it didn't really solve them.

"Life is moving all around us." Storm jumped up, dissolved into mist, and vanished. *"Don't get left behind!"* Her voice seemed to hang in the air where she had been sitting only a moment before.

Adriane leaped to her feet and went after her friend, more determined than ever to be strong. Maybe in the process she'd discover something all her own. A place where she truly belonged.

2

*W*HERE WAS THAT wolf hiding? Adriane skidded to a stop at the edge of a large clearing. The size of a football field and ringed by magnificent oaks and pines, the field rustled with the wispy sigh of meadow grass and wildflowers.

This was the field where they'd discovered the portal, hidden by magic they could not yet control. Closing her eyes and concentrating hard, she held up her braceleted arm and moved slowly in a circle, scanning the trees, thinking not of the jewel itself but of what she wanted it to help her do. Focus on Storm, her friend.

The wolf stone sparked to life with an amber glow.

The sharp image of crystal-blue water flashed in Adriane's mind. Mirror Lake.

"I've got you," she called out, laughing.

"Then come and get me." The wolf's voice filled her mind.

Adriane stepped into the field, focusing on Storm's image—

—*Flash*—

The wolf stone flared with light as the forest faded around her.

Holding up her wrist, Adriane spun in a circle. "Storm, I'm going to find you," she called out.

Trees swept past her field of vision in a blur—

—*Flash*—

She felt the soft padding of paws hitting the hard earth in long strides.

Adriane pushed hard, closing her eyes, and the wolf stone blazed with light—

—*Flash*—

The sudden smell of damp wood filled her nose; the leaves beneath her feet felt cool and damp.

Feeling the magical connection grow, Adriane willed herself with all her might to find her friend—

—it was as if a door suddenly flew open.

She opened her eyes and every detail of the forest came into sharp focus. Adriane staggered, overwhelmed with sights and sounds, tastes and smells, sensations unlike anything she had ever experienced. It was as if she no longer was in her own body. She was low to the ground, mighty muscles corded and taut, ready to leap and run with the strength of a wolf.

She *was* a wolf, running free, the wolfsong filling her heart with a power she had never dreamed possible.

"Storm!" she cried out.

Two wild hearts beat as one, a hunter without prey, a warrior without purpose, a lone wolf without a family, never to hear the yelps of pups, the last of her kind.

Caught in a whirlwind of feelings she could not control, Adriane threw back her head and howled. The sound tore from her throat, feral and wild, echoing through the forests and beyond.

Before her, the portal in the field swirled open. How could it have opened? The sparkling dreamcatcher hung in front of the portal, floating in the air before a spinning tunnel of stars.

From somewhere across the astral planes, the wolfsong answered her call.

Head lowered, Adriane turned and saw a mistwolf shimmer into existence. A huge black wolf stood in the field. He raised his black-ruffed head and howled.

Could this really be *another* mistwolf? Was Storm not the last of her kind?

Adriane ran toward him. "Who are you?" she called out.

The wolf backed away, the fur of his ruff standing out threateningly. Fiery golden eyes narrowed and stared as she approached.

"I am Moonshadow, pack leader of the mistwolves. Who dares to call the wolf pack?" The wolf's lip curled, revealing long, sharp teeth.

Adriane stopped short. "I am packmate to a mistwolf."

The wolf snarled, then tensed, ready to strike. *"Humans do not belong with mistwolves."*

As if possessed, Adriane snarled back, an inhuman cry. Her stone flashed golden fire on her wrist and she instinctively leaped for the wolf.

Silver mist flashed in front of her and Storm appeared, teeth bared.

The two wolves faced each other.

"Stand aside, the human has challenged me," the strange mistwolf called.

Storm glared fiercely at the other wolf. *"She is my pack-mate. Her fight is my fight."*

"You belong with us," the pack leader said, a strange sadness to his tone.

"You cannot be real. There are no others."

The giant black wolf threw back his head and howled. Behind him, dozens of mistwolves appeared from the portal. Blue, black, white, silver, golden, female, male, and pup, they stood looking at Storm. Suddenly, they lifted their heads and howled as one.

Storm answered. And the wolfsong filled the field.

Adriane wanted to feel it, to share it with her friend. She threw her head back and howled with them. The wolves suddenly fell silent and faced the girl.

Adriane stifled her howl, self-consciously aware that she was not a part of the pack.

"This is a time of peril for all mistwolves," the pack leader said to Storm. *"You must run with us now."*

Adriane's world began to crumble. She understood the joy that filled Storm's heart and the white-hot fear that filled her own.

Storm locked eyes with her. *"I must follow the call of the wolfsong."*

Adriane lowered her head.

"Be strong, warrior."

Adriane felt tears running down her face. "Take me with you."

"That is not possible," the pack leader said. *"The mistwolf belongs with her own kind."*

Adriane felt numb. How could she stand in the way of her friend discovering the most important thing in her life? If Storm left, she'd feel deserted by her best friend. If she made Storm stay, she'd feel worse. She braced herself—Storm went to stand by the pack leader.

"Remember." Storm's golden eyes gazed warmly at Adriane. *"You found me once. You will always find me."*

Without a backward glance, all the wolves drifted into mist and swept through the portal. The portal swirled closed behind them, and vanished. Adriane let the pain wash over her as she howled in the empty field, alone.

3

"ARE YOU SURE there are no snakes here?" Heather's voice trembled as the redhead gingerly picked her way down the trail.

"Maybe there's pythons!" Joey ran up behind Molly and pretended to choke her. "They sneak up and crush you to pieces!"

"Ewwww. Stop that, Joey!" Molly squealed and ducked behind Kara, knocking into their blond tour guide.

"Dude." Marcus laughed. "Pythons only live in, like, South America."

"The Ravenswood Wildlife Preserve is home to many different species of animals, but we haven't seen any snakes." Kara Davies' voice carried over the group as they made their way from the Mist Trail into Wolf Run Pass. Kara's friends, Heather, Tiffany, Molly, Joey, and Marcus, followed their intrepid tour guide through the lush forest.

"Where's the dinosaur bush?" Joey asked.

Marcus mock-punched his friend. "Dude, that might be too scary for you."

Kara scanned the map that folded out from her notebook. "The hedge animals are in the topiary gardens."

"You should have, like, bear wrestling," Joey suggested.

"Man, I'd pay to see that!" Marcus jostled Joey as he roared like a bear.

"You are so immature," Tiffany scolded. "There's no more bears here."

A growl from the deep, dense forests answered back.

"What was that?" Heather nervously looked around.

"Well, this *is* an animal preserve," Kara said slyly. "If we're lucky, we'll see some wild animals through Wolf Run Pass."

"Are you sure this is safe?" Molly moved close behind Tiffany and Heather as the group entered a wide glade surrounded by large, moss-covered rocks and trees on either side.

"Ravenswood is a natural habitat for animals." Kara waved her arms and called out dramatically, "You never know what might drop in!"

Her friends looked at each other, puzzled.

"Aerobics?" Tiffany asked.

Heather shrugged.

"Ooo, I think I hear something," Kara carefully called out again.

Suddenly a shadow passed overhead as a large, flying creature circled the group.

"What's that?" Molly squealed.

"It's a bird—" Joey started

"It's a plane—" Marcus continued.

Heather crossed her arms. "It's an owl, you morons."

Ariel gently landed on Kara's outstretched arm, her wing feathers shimmering with purple-and-turquoise sparkles.

"A great snow owl. Hi, Ariel," Kara, beaming, said to the owl. "These are my friends that have come to meet you."

The owl surveyed the group with huge turquoise eyes. "Hoo doo yooo doo."

"Hey, that owl almost sounds like it talks," Joey said.

"You are so silly. Animals don't talk," Tiffany scoffed.

"Yeah, pretty silly," Kara remarked, scratching Ariel's head.

"I was chasing a mouse."

"No eating during showtime," Kara whispered, quickly nuzzling her cheek on the owl before gently releasing Ariel to fly away.

The group pressed forward down the trail.

"What other mighty creatures of the forests might be out here?" Kara asked dramatically.

A ferocious roar split the air.

Molly jumped. "What was that?"

"Shhh, look!" Kara whispered, pointing.

Before the group, perched on a large pile of rocks, was a big, spotted cat. Her lustrous fur shone orange with black spots.

"It's the leopard!" Heather yelped.

"Run!" Joey shouted, taking a step backward.

Kara stepped forward. "If we all stay real quiet, I think I can pet her."

"Are you crazy?!" Molly whispered.

The big cat jumped down to stand in front of Kara as she slowly reached out and moved closer.

"Kara, be careful . . ." Heather bit her lip.

Over her shoulder, Kara whispered to her friends. "If I just act friendly, maybe she won't eat me . . . I hope." She winked at Lyra. The big cat winked back.

"Kara! This is *so* not funny!" Tiffany called out, stamping her foot.

As Kara approached, the wild animal crouched low and gave a fierce growl.

"Ahhhhh!" Everyone screamed, falling over one another as they tried to run away.

With her back to her friends, Kara bent over, inspecting the cat's fur. "You need a bath," she said, examining the cat's ears.

"I do not. I smell like wildflowers," Lyra replied casually.

She gave the cat a quick kiss. "You got the wild part right."

"It's beauty and the beast," Marcus cracked as the cat scrambled up the rocks and back into the woods.

"Hey, that's a good one, Marcus." Kara quickly scribbled in her notebook.

"You scared us half to death!" Tiffany pouted.

"C'mon," Kara laughed. "I'll show you the lawn behind the manor where we're planning the benefit concert."

"Great tour, Kara!" Joey said, grinning.

"Ka-ra! Ka-ra! Ka-ra!" they chanted, heading down the trail.

A mournful howl stopped their chant. It came from behind a vine-covered opening between the trees.

"All right! A bear!" Marcus said excitedly.

Joey mock-punched his friend again.

The cry rose again.

"Oo, oo, me, me, my turn," Tiffany yelled. "I want to pet the animals, too." She skipped over to the vines.

"Hey, that's not part of the tour," Kara muttered, checking her notes.

"Here I am, cute thing." Tiffany slowly pulled the leaves aside and screamed.

Adriane stood, eyes glazed, dirt streaked and smeared across her face. From her hiking boots to her black jeans and up to her pullover sweater and forest-green vest, she was covered in mud, leaves, and grass stains.

"Oh, it's just you," Tiffany said.

Adriane eyed the group from behind straggly, damp black hair.

"What happened, you fall in a marsh bog?" Joey called out, walking over.

"Leave me alone," Adriane snarled, stumbling away.

The boy stepped back. "Hey, easy. I was only trying to help."

"She is sooo weird," Tiffany whispered to Heather.

"Yeah, even weirder than normal," Heather agreed.

Kara walked over to Adriane. "What's up?" She eyed Adriane more closely. "You look awful."

"Leave me alone," Adriane repeated and turned away.

"Hey, is she okay?" Marcus asked as Kara's friends moved in closer for a better look.

Suddenly, Ariel dove from the sky to land on Adriane's arm. The owl leaned into Adriane's neck, cooing softly and nuzzling her cheek.

"What's the matter with her?" Molly asked.

"Cat's got her tongue?" Heather quipped.

With a loud hiss, Lyra jumped to Adriane's side, standing protectively close.

"Keep away from her," the cat growled.

Kara's friends understood the cat's actions perfectly, even if they couldn't hear the words.

"Okay, okay, everyone back off," Kara ordered. "Head back to the main road. I'll be there in a minute."

When her friends had moved out of earshot, Kara turned quickly to Lyra. "What is it? What's wrong?"

"Stormbringer is gone," Lyra told her.

"Oh, that wolf is always wandering around," Kara laughed, picking leaves and twigs from Adriane's hair. "She'll probably be back in a few hours."

"No, the mistwolf is gone," the cat repeated.

Kara searched Adriane's eyes. They were red and puffy, streaked with tears.

"What do you mean, gone?" Kara asked.

Adriane pressed the owl and the cat close to her. "She's gone," she stated simply.

"Lyra," Kara said to the cat, "take her to Emily. I'll join you as fast as I can."

She gripped Adriane's arms and looked in her eyes. "Adriane, go with Lyra and Ariel. Okay?"

"Come on, Adriane, just hold on to me," Lyra said, leading Adriane down the path to the manor house. Adriane stumbled after her, silently calling for Storm and hearing nothing.

∞

EMILY FLETCHER BLEW a loose auburn curl off her face and clicked on the icon to open the Ravenswood mailbox. She turned from her computer to a second workstation set up on a table next to her desk.

"Mail call," she announced. "It's from Meilin."

Ozzie, a golden brown ferret, sat on three pillows pecking away on the keyboard. Ronif, a quiffle, sat behind him as Balthazar, a pegasus, stood watching carefully. They were busy working on their secret database of magic and magical animals. After all, they actually had firsthand knowledge of these creatures, being magical themselves! Although technically an elf, Ozzie was determined that just because he was stuck in a ferret body, it didn't mean he had to act like one. At least not in front of his friends.

"Don't forget to include that they have bad breath," Ronif commented, flapping his rubbery beak over Ozzie's shoulder.

"Pe-yew! Believe you me" Ozzie remarked, "when there's a kobold in the neighborhood, you know it!"

Emily smiled proudly at her team. She turned back and opened the email.

Meilin lived in Shanghai, China. She and Emily had become good friends in the past month, trading emails and info about animals and legends. Meilin's father was an archeologist who used to tell her stories of great and powerful dragons. Meilin wanted to know whether Emily believed in dragons.

"Well, team magic," Emily asked her animal friends. "Dragons, real or myth?"

"Real, of course. Why wouldn't they be?" Balthazar answered.

After all the magical animals they'd seen here at Ravenswood, a dragon wouldn't be that far-fetched. Emily thought of Phelonius, a creature so magical he couldn't survive on Earth. He'd helped her find the courage to use her healing magic. He was the most amazing creature she had ever seen. And if she hadn't seen him with her own two eyes, she never would've believed *he* was real. So why couldn't dragons be real, too?

"You've seen one then?" Emily asked.

"*I* haven't, personally." Ozzie gestured with his furry paws. "But Cousin Schmoot had this friend who knew this troll whose brother-in-law had this neighbor whose cousin was a warlock who used to go to school with this dwarf whose grandmother swore on her deathbed that one time when she was little she had seen a real, live dragon!"

"I see . . ." Emily laughed. "How could I ever have doubted it?"

"Dragons are very rare and powerful magical creatures," Balthazar said. "They have long been extinct on Aldenmor." He looked up suddenly. "Lyra's here."

"How's Kara's tour go—" Ronif started to ask.

Lyra padded in, nudging Adriane along as if she were a rag doll.

"Adriane! What happened?" Emily was across the room and by her friend's side in an instant. "Ozzie! Get me some damp towels!"

Ozzie dropped to the floor and scampered off as Emily led her friend to a leather couch and sat her down.

Adriane was covered in caked mud and sticky leaves.

"Are you all right? Are you hurt?" Emily asked, eyes full of concern.

Fresh tears ran down Adriane's cheeks.

"What happened?" Emily repeated.

"Here, Adriane." Ronif handed her a water bottle.

Adriane took a long drink. "Thank you."

Ozzie returned with the cool, damp towels and Emily carefully wiped the dried mud and leaves from her friend's face, checking for bruises or cuts.

"Feeling better?"

"No." Adriane then launched into a breathless recap of what had happened out in the field, sobbing as her emotions overwhelmed her.

"She's gone, Emily!" Adriane finished, blinking away her tears.

"But Storm is the last mistwolf," Balthazar said, puzzled.

"Storm always thought she was the last of her kind. Can you imagine what she felt like, learning there were others?" Ozzie said.

"I know," Adriane sniffled. "But it's not safe there! I shouldn't have let her go."

"It wasn't your choice to make, Adriane," Emily said gently.

"We've been practicing to see how far away we could talk to each other. If I could use my wolf stone, maybe I could talk to her."

"But she's in Aldenmor," Emily said. "How could you—you're not thinking of opening the portal?"

"I have to know that she's all right."

"We've never been able to open it on command," Emily reminded her.

"Somehow Storm and I made it work."

"Sounds like it was opened from the other side," Balthazar pointed out

"There's got to be a way," Adriane insisted.

"I don't know . . ."

"Hey, kids! What's all the drama?" Kara walked into the library, pulling her golden hair back in a ponytail.

Ozzie regarded Kara. "There might be a way to open the portal," he said slowly.

The others all followed his gaze.

Kara stopped, a suspicious look crossing her face. "What?"

4

"*M*AGIC ATTRACTS MAGIC." Ozzie was pacing in the grass, reviewing the plan. "And we know the dragonflies have different magic. They pop in and out without a portal, and they wove Kara's hair into the dreamcatcher. Ergo, the dragonflies may be able to open it!" Ozzie opened his forepaws triumphantly, as if waiting for applause.

Adriane, Emily, and Kara stood in the empty field, listening.

"It seems like the safest way to open the portal. Let the dragonflies do it," Emily agreed.

Kara was not thrilled with this plan. She looked around furtively and shuddered, remembering her *hair-owing* experience not so long ago with the tiny dragons.

They adored Kara, but she'd finally managed to convince the pesky things to stop driving her crazy by popping in and out all over the place. Well, if she had to do this, at least Heather, Molly, Tiffany, Joey, and Marcus weren't here to witness it. Her school friends had gone home. They didn't know about the magic, yet.

"If the portal opens," Emily said to Adriane, "try to use your stone to make contact with Storm."

Adriane looked determined. "Ready."

Emily and Adriane stood on either side of Kara and held up their wrists. Kara always made the other girls' magic stronger when she helped them. Now she extended her arms, touching Emily and Adriane's gemstones.

Emily's rainbow jewel and Adriane's wolf stone began to glow. Halos of blue-green and amber light danced around Kara's fingers then jumped up her arms, swirling around her body.

"Okay, Kara, call the dragonflies," Emily prompted.

"Do I have to?" Kara complained.

The others looked at her.

"All right, all right." Kara took a deep breath, sighed, and called out in a singsong voice, "Yoo-hoo! Dragonflies! Barney, Goldie, Fred, Fiona, Blaze, where are you? Ollie ollie oxen free!"

"Ollie ollie oxen free?' Ozzie was stumped. "I haven't heard that magical spell before."

"Picture them in your minds," Emily instructed.

Kara closed her eyes and pictured the bird-sized dragons. "Come out, come out, wherever you are!" she called.

Suddenly the air began to sparkle.

Pop! Pop! Pop! Pop! Pop!

Multicolored bubbles burst like small fireworks as a swarm of dragonflies popped in. The girls dropped their arms and stepped back.

"Kaaraa!" a golden dragonfly called out, swooping down to land on Kara's shoulder.

"Watch the hair!" she yelled.

Barney, the purple one, landed belly down on Ozzie's head, hanging over to stare into the startled ferret's face. "Oozzook!"

"Gah! Get away, you!"

"Shh, Ozzie, don't scare them," Emily warned.

The mini dragons flitted around Kara, jabbering excitedly, all angling to get closest to her.

"Yes, yes, you found me," Kara said. "Hooray for you." Purple Barney, red Fiona, yellow Goldie, blue Fred, and orange Blaze all began to dive and spin around the girls, pinwheeling and squeaking.

"Kara, get them under control!" Adriane said impatiently.

"I'm trying!" Kara batted the pesky creatures away.

"Try a gentler approach," Emily suggested.

"Hey!" Kara yelled. "Listen up!"

"Ooo!" The dragonflies stopped in mid-twirl, hovering in front of her.

"Instead of playing our regular 'Throw the Shoe at the Dragonflies' game that you all love so much, I have a special *new* game for us to play." The dragonflies twittered in anticipation. "It's called the 'Open the Portal' game! Yay!" The dragonflies twirled and squealed.

"We want to see the beautiful web you made for us," Emily told them.

"Ooo, Emee." Fiona nuzzled Emily's hair.

"Show us the web, Goldie. You remember." Kara pointed to her blond hair in front of the hovering golden dragonfly. "The web you made from my hair."

The five dragonflies buzzed into action. Forming a circle, they locked tiny claws together and began to spin. They spun faster, filling the air with colorful bursts of light.

"That's it!" Adriane exclaimed.

Faster and faster they spun as hundreds of bubbles popped like fireworks. Wind began to whip through the field as the air churned, boiling with color.

"Something's happening!" Emily called out.

Suddenly the bubbles all merged. The girls and Ozzie shielded their eyes as intense light filled the field. The light faded, revealing a circle of shimmering stars hanging just off the ground—the portal.

In front of the portal hung the sparkling dream-catcher. It was just the way they had left it: rainbow-colored strands of Kara's hair still woven into a large, glistening web of protection—a dreamcatcher, designed to block evil magic from entering Ravenswood.

"They did it!" Ozzie yelled triumphantly.

"Hurry, before it closes!" Emily urged Adriane.

Adriane gazed at the huge dreamcatcher hanging in the sky. She held up her wolf stone and pictured Storm in her mind. "Storm . . . can you hear me?" she whispered. She concentrated harder. "Stormbringer?"

"Anything?" Emily asked.

"No, I can't get through."

"Try again," Kara said.

"Storm? It's me, Adriane!"

The web trembled, but she still couldn't feel anything. "It's not working!" she cried, frustrated.

"The dreamcatcher may be interfering with reception," Ozzie ventured.

Adriane quickly turned to Kara. "Get the dragonflies to open it."

"I don't know if that's such a good idea," Ozzie said.

"Please!" Adriane pleaded.

Emily nodded at Kara.

"D-flies, listen up!" Kara called. The dragonflies all zoomed over to hover around Kara. "We need you to open the web, okay? On your mark . . . Get set . . . Go!"

The dragonflies immediately flew to the top of the dreamcatcher, grabbing strands of webbing in their beaks.

"What are they doing?" Emily asked.

"How should I know?" Kara shrugged. "I'm amazed they understand anything I say at all."

Each holding a strand of hair, the dragonflies pulled the dreamcatcher down, making it spin end over end. It whirled hypnotically before the misty portal.

Adriane held up her stone and focused. This time she sensed a faint glimmer—a connection. Storm? "I felt something!" Adriane said excitedly.

"I think that's amplifying the signal," Ozzie observed.

The dragonflies began to slow down and Adriane's connection faded.

"Keep the dragonflies spinning!" she called out.

"How am I supposed to do that?" Kara asked.

"Hurry, the portal is closing!" Ozzie waved his paws in the air.

Adriane saw the tunnel swirling into a tighter spiral, drawing the edges of the portal toward the center.

Kara eyed the dragonflies' formation carefully. Bobbing her head in time with their motions, she watched the moving strands sweep over the ground and past her. She used to be really good at this game.

With one swift leap Kara jumped into the throng of dragonflies and start skipping over the moving strands.

The dragonflies all squealed with delight at this new game and began spinning faster, around and around.

Adriane felt the magic connection again, stronger—

—*Flash!*—

Crystal towers loomed over scorched earth, pulsing green—

—*Flash!*—

A dark dungeon filled with sick animals—

Adriane leaned in closer . . .

—*Flash!*—

A lone mistwolf crying for its lost human.

Adriane gasped. "Storm?"

"*You are always in my heart.*" The voice was so faint it might have been a whisper. It might have been the wind.

It was hard to stay focused with all the commotion going on, with the web spinning, dragonflies buzzing around, and Kara singing, "Miss Mary Mack, Mack, Mack! All dressed in black, black, black! With silver buttons, buttons, buttons! All down her back, back, back!"

Adriane tried to ignore all the distractions and concentrate the way Storm had taught her: to focus on what she was trying to accomplish—to control the magic, get it to do exactly what she wanted. And what Adriane wanted more than anything at this moment was Storm by her side. She squeezed her eyes tightly shut. "*Stormbringer!*"

The starry lights of the portal dimmed with an eerie glow.

Tendrils of magic touched her mind, tentatively probing.

The dreamcatcher whipped around and around Kara, who jumped and ducked and did everything she could to keep from getting tagged.

The connection pulled at Adriane's magic, coaxing her. She reached out, grasping for some clarity, fighting to hold it, and felt . . . an animal? A human? She was confused. The magic suddenly locked tight as a vise.

"Agh!" Adriane recoiled in pain.

"Adriane?" Emily called out.

The dreamcatcher was trembling violently. Kara frantically jump-roped as if her life depended on it.

Adriane was jerked forward with a tremendous force. "Ahh!"

"Adriane! What is it?" Emily's voice sounded so far away.

"I'm being pulled in!" Something had latched onto the magic of Adriane's jewel and was dragging her toward the center of the portal.

"Whatever you're doing, Kara, cut it out!" she screamed, trying to calm her growing fear by focusing on a far more familiar emotion: being annoyed at Kara. "Call off the dragonflies!"

"Pook?"

Kara had jumped free. All the dragonflies clustered around her. They were no longer holding on to the dreamcatcher. "Uh-oh."

The web was spinning on its own, vibrating wildly at odd angles.

Sproing! One by one, the strands began to snap.

"This can't be good," Ozzie said.

Emily grabbed Adriane by the waist, trying to hold her back. "Help!" she screamed as her sneakers slid through the soft grass.

"Emily!" Ozzie yelled, hopping up and down.

Adriane felt the wind whip at her back as two large wings flapped behind her. Lyra had her front paws wrapped around Emily, her golden wings unfurled and beating against the force that pulled them forward.

Ozzie grabbed the cat's tail and pulled with all his might.

"Kookie!"

The dragonflies darted behind Ozzie. Goldie grabbed one of Ozzie's rear paws in her beak, pulling the ferret up in the air. Fred grabbed onto Goldie's tail. Each dragonfly pulled on the tail of the one before it, forming a line, their little wings beating furiously.

"Go, go, go!" Kara jumped up and down, cheering them on.

"Pull!" Emily yelled.

Suddenly, long strands of hair sprang out in all directions as the dreamcatcher unraveled. A blinding sunburst filled the field as the strands were sucked into the portal and disappeared.

Emily, Ozzie, Lyra and the dragonflies all tumbled backward, piling on top of Kara.

Adriane went tumbling forward, headfirst.

"Get off me!" Kara pushed the pile of animals away and scrambled to her feet.

The field was quiet. The portal was gone. Everything was back to normal . . . except for one thing.

Kara and Emily looked at each other in shock, speaking at the same time.

"Where's Adriane?"

5

IT WASN'T SO much a sensation of falling. It was more like flying, drifting in a dream. Adriane was surrounded by a golden glow, as if she were inside a bubble of light. She couldn't tell which way was up. Through the glow, she could make out what looked like rivers of stars.

Shapes came into focus. She was skimming over a cratered surface. Then she saw trees, a forest landscape.

"Humm-hamm-hamuckamuck!"

The strange sound rose in the distance.

"Hamma-doo-wark!"

Someone was singing, or at least trying to sing. It sounded more like a bullfrog croaking. She squinted, straining to make out any shapes through the golden light.

"Humm-dumm-dokkarrood!"

The singing was getting louder.

Adriane fell with a stomach-lurching drop and hit the ground—

"SPLAAGfooF!" The singing stopped.

—hard.

Well, not that hard. Something soft and mushy had broken her fall. The golden light faded, leaving a faint afterglow, matching the glow from her wolf stone.

The sky above was a milky gray. All was still.

She sat up and surveyed her surroundings. Maybe she didn't fall through the portal after all. Wide-open woods spread around her, not too different from Ravenswood. But as her eyes adjusted to the gray light, she realized that the trees—what few were still standing— were covered in a thick, tar-like muck. What looked like hanging moss at first was, upon closer inspection, rubbery, moldy, black seaweed choking the trees. The ground was damp with not a blade of grass in sight. Not a *color* in sight! Unless you count gray as a color. She shivered as it hit her: she *had* fallen through the portal. She was not on Earth anymore, and she was totally alone.

"Mmmmfff!"

Something cold and clammy was squirming in the mud right underneath her! Adriane screamed and leaped to her feet.

Something kicked its way out of the soft dirt.

"Who is you that rained on me?" the creature sniveled, shaking off dirt and mud like a dog.

"Huh?" She must've fallen out of the sky right on top of this creature. Adriane stood with her wrist raised, breathing fast. The wolf stone pulsed with golden light, reacting to her distress.

The thing began feeling around in the dirt, searching for something as its large round eyes found Adriane and widened in terror. "A witch!" It fell back over its own big feet and groveled in the dirt. "I am only humble Scorge. Do not turn me to stone, O Witch!" it wailed.

"I'm not a witch. I'm sorry. You frightened me," Adriane said, watching the creature warily.

"I frightened you?" The creature smiled, showing rows of little pointy teeth. "Must be very poor witch."

It stood up. It was sort of apelike in appearance, hunched, with long arms. Its short orange fur on those parts that weren't covered in mud made it look like a deranged orangutan.

"Uh . . . I'm sorry I landed on you, um, sir. My name's Adriane. Are you all right?"

"No! Me is not *All right!* Me is Scorge." The creature began frantically looking around again.

"You made Scorge lose big magic stone." He stopped, seeing Adriane's jewel. "Soooo . . ." The creature pointed a stubby finger at her wrist. "That means you must give Scorge magic stone."

Adriane's gem was softly pulsing with light. "I don't think so."

"You not from around here . . ." Scorge moved toward Adriane and her jewel.

"No, I'm from . . . over the rainbow," Adriane said, backing away.

"Where is this rainbow place, near Moorgroves perhaps?" it asked slyly.

"Uh, maybe. You just stay away from me now."

"Scorge need magic stone!" The creature charged at Adriane.

Before Adriane could react, her jewel exploded with power. A beam of searing gold light shot out at Scorge, knocking the creature fifteen feet in the air.

"Oooowahhh!"

"Oh, I'm so sorry!" Adriane ran over to the downed creature. She hadn't meant to use such force—the jewel had just reacted. "Are you okay?"

"No! No! No! Me Scorge!" He shook his furry head. "Me thinks Scorge don't want that jewel."

He got up, hanging his orange head in defeat.

This was not the best way to make friends in a brand-new world, Adriane thought. "Maybe I can help you find your stone," she suggested.

"Must find stone!" Scorge lifted his head, his big eyes lighting up. "Get big reward!"

"I think it might have rolled that way." Adriane pointed to a shallow gully in the dirt that traveled up and over a hill behind them . . . although she was fairly certain a rock didn't roll uphill.

Scorge scurried up the hill in the direction his "magic stone" had rolled, desperate to catch up to it. "Scorge get big reward for big stone!" He glowered back at Adriane, then tripped over his big feet and fell over the ridge, disappearing down the other side.

A great big magic stone? Adriane thought to herself, tapping her own stone in the bracelet on her wrist. Could this Scorge really have a giant-sized magic stone? She had to be careful. The magic seemed much more powerful here, and dangerous.

"GaooahooHoo!"

Scorge's cry came from over the hill. Adriane looked around. If no one had heard Scorge's horrendous screaming by now, there probably wasn't anyone else nearby. Sighing, she carefully walked up the hill.

Adriane peeked cautiously over and saw an empty riverbed. Scorge's dilemma became all too clear: the riverbed was filled with hundreds of identical muddy, gray rocks. She was startled as Scorge suddenly burst out sobbing uncontrollably.

"Oh, me face! Baddest luck finded Scorge!" he bawled. "Me, me, me!"

He was so pathetic. Despite how rude he'd been to her, Adriane felt sorry for him.

She got an idea. "Hey, maybe I can help you find it," she called out, walking down toward him.

Scorge looked up, wary, but still crying.

Stepping into the riverbed, Adriane held out her gem-stone, moving it carefully over the large rocks. She didn't even know if this would work, but as Ozzie had told them, magic attracts magic.

Adriane's wolf stone was beginning to pulse. She continued to wave it across the muddy riverbed when suddenly one of the many gray rocks began to pulse a dull, dirty light. "Look, Scorge!"

Scorge ceased his crying. "Ooo!"

He lumbered over and gleefully bent, kissing the big stone over and over again. Adriane flinched as she watched him kiss a rock covered in dried mud and goo.

"So, now that I helped you, maybe you can help me, huh?" Adriane hoped she wasn't pressing her luck.

Scorge stopped in mid-smooch. "What witch want from Scorge?" He gazed suspiciously at her and hugged the rock close.

"Where am I?" Adriane asked. "What is this place?"

"Pooowa." He spit out some dirt. "You never heard of the Shadowlands?"

Adriane gasped. The Shadowlands. This was a place of terrible danger. This was where Lyra escaped from that sorceress. The cat had been burned by the Black Fire poison here. This was where the manticore came from! She shivered. This was not good at all. Was Storm somewhere in the Shadowlands, too? Or had the mistwolf ended up somewhere else?

"GraaaK!!" Scorge was trying to lift the rock, but it wouldn't budge. He toppled over it instead. He got up and tried again, and fell over the immobile stone. This time he got up and kicked it with his big toe.

"OOhhhAAAA!"

That didn't work. That rock wasn't moving.

"What you do to magic stone?" Scorge yelled, hopping around, holding a swollen toe.

"I didn't do anything."

"Rock schtuck!"

Adriane gazed out at the desolate landscape beyond the riverbed. "How do I get out of here? Which way do I go?"

"Me don't care what way witch goes!" Scorge said angrily. "Me go get imps. They move stone with big magic. Make bad witch disappear!"

Imps? What are those? She shuddered.

Before Adriane could stop him, Scorge scampered off down the ravine without looking back and was gone.

A wave of fear swept over Adriane. Steady, she told herself. As much as she didn't want to, she knew she had to move. Although there was no sign of the glowing green poison that was called Black Fire, she knew it was here. All around her, the landscape was harsh, bleak, completely barren. Dark patterns instead of clouds swirled eerily in the sky, constantly in motion. It felt to Adriane like the land itself was trying to breathe, gasping for air. She had to find Storm and get out of here.

But Storm could be anywhere! She felt panic rising.

"Calm down!" she said aloud. She hugged herself, then exhaled deeply. One hand found the wolf stone on her wrist, and she instantly felt better. It was probably a good idea to go in the opposite direction from Scorge. Whatever imps were, she didn't want to wait around and find out.

Adriane held the wolf stone out, and, as if in response, a glow ignited, slowly swirling in its center. Gazing into the amber light, Adriane concentrated as hard as she could on Storm. She imagined leaning against Storm's soft fur. She relived, in her mind, the quiet moments they had spent together.

"Storm, where are you?"

The wolf stone suddenly flashed. A burning white-gold light washed out Adriane's vision completely. She felt as if she were being pulled through some kind of tunnel at a breakneck speed, zooming past hazy images she could not decipher. Cloudy shapes began to form in front of her. Dozens of figures slowly came into view, all four-legged creatures, silhouetted on a lush green hillside.

Lush green? Adriane hazily became aware that she was looking upon a forested, mountain landscape, when a moment before all around her had been barren and gray. Mistwolves paced back and forth. She could smell them and hear them. And she was among them. She was one of them!

Storm?

Where was Stormbringer? Adriane looked carefully at each mistwolf. None was familiar. Suddenly she recognized the big, black wolf she had seen in the portal—Moonshadow, the pack leader. He sniffed the air, then turned sharp golden eyes on her.

Adriane gasped.

The huge wolf spoke directly to her. *"Stormbringer! Let the human go."*

Stormbringer! He had called *her* Stormbringer! No, Adriane realized, she was seeing through Storm's eyes!

Suddenly the connection was cut off, as if someone had just hung up the phone.

The searing glow of Adriane's jewel faded, and the greenery around her gave way to gray. Adriane was again standing in the same muddy riverbed where Scorge had left her.

She had been in Storm's mind—seen through her eyes and saw that Storm had her real family now. Even so, Adriane refused to believe that Storm would ever turn her back on her.

Adriane squinted. More gray forests, rolling into hills . . . and, in the distance, she could make out snow-covered peaks of a mountain range.

That was where she had to go—she could only trust in the magic to guide her.

Adriane walked out of the riverbed in the direction of the mountains. They had to be a good ten miles away.

Something *clunked* behind her.

Adriane whirled around. But all was quiet.

She turned back and took a few steps, when she heard a clattering in the rocks.

She turned again, her senses on high alert. "Who's there?" She scanned the riverbed. "Scorge?" No answer.

Then she heard it again.

"Whoever you are, I know you're there! Show yourself!"

Adriane's heart pounded in her throat. She flashed on the nightmare vision of the manticore. That monster had terrorized the animals at Ravenswood until she, Emily, and Kara had sent it back through the portal—maybe right back here.

She heard a short rattle and froze. Then one large, oval rock, the size of a beach ball, shook back and forth.

"Huh?"

The mud-crusted rock teetered among the other gray rocks . . . and fell over. It wobbled and then slowly began to roll *itself!*

Adriane's jaw dropped. She watched in amazement as the rock gingerly toddled toward her and came to a stop at her feet.

"Hello," Adriane said awkwardly. "Great. I'm talking to a rock."

The rock rattled and shook and settled back at her feet.

"So you're, like, just a rock?" The rock said nothing. "Well, I'd love to stay and chat, but I've got to roll."

Adriane turned and began to walk away. The rock rolled after her. She stopped. The rock stopped. "I guess you didn't like Scorge, either," she said over her shoulder. The rock said nothing.

She started walking away again. This time she was pretty sure what to expect. She smiled when she heard the gravelly rattle behind her. Without looking back, she said conversationally, "Well, it is a nice day for a stroll—er, roll? You from around here? I'm just visiting."

Adriane began the long hike from the riverbed up into the desolate forest. She realized she was actually grateful for the company of the rock, and found it comforting, even. I guess this must be a pet rock, she chuckled to herself.

"Is that what you are, Rocky? A pet rock?" She leaned down and rubbed the rock playfully. It rolled in a happy little figure eight around Adriane's feet. "Yes, you are! Who's a good widdle pet rock? You! That's who!" If the rock had a tail, she was sure it'd be wagging it right now. Just wait until she showed it to the others—a pang of homesickness swept over her.

Adriane had been trying not to think about that. She wasn't exactly sure how she was going to get home. And what if she was *never* able to get home? No, don't even go there! Panicking wouldn't do her—or Storm—any good. She had to stay focused on the task at hand, as Storm had taught her.

"I have a friend here. I'm on my way to find her,"

Adriane explained as they continued to walk past dark and forbidding woods. "She's my best friend in the world—my world, anyway. You ever have a friend like that?"

The rock shuddered and rolled on top of her foot.

Adriane stopped and looked down. "Well, you have one now."

The rock rolled around Adriane's feet.

She brushed brambles out of their way as she pushed through small patches of fog, winding around dead trees, following the soft, golden halo of the wolf stone. Finally Adriane realized they were leaving the vicinity of the gray forest. Green grass was beginning to show in patches. Cold wind swept her hair as they crested a steep incline and looked at a series of mist-covered valleys before them. Adriane could see the tops of rocky cliffs, then foothills, and beyond them loomed the crystalline mountains.

"This is not the way I imaged Aldenmor to be," she mused. "Ravenswood is so beautiful. This is such a cold and frightening place."

The rock rolled silently by her feet.

"You're a really good listener, you know that?" Adriane was glad to have the rocky hitchhiker along for the journey. With it by her side, she felt a little less alone in this strange and scary world.

She didn't see the giant flying creature and its rider circling overhead, watching her every move.

6

"LET'S ROCK AND roll!" Adriane called out. The rock was moving in big circles as they made their way down a steep hill in lazy, sprawling zigzag patterns. The rock ambled along, zigging as she zagged.

"Hey, you're pretty good." Adriane laughed as the rock twirled past like a graceful skater. "C'mon! Race ya to the top!" She took off up the next hill.

The rock spun around and with a burst of speed, plowed straight past her, right to the crest of the hill.

"No fair!" Adriane called out. "You rocked *and* rolled!" She laughed.

The rock stood frozen in place at the top of the hill.

Then it began shaking, spun around, and rolled back to Adriane, hiding behind her legs. It was quivering in fear.

Adriane's guard went up. "What's wrong? What is it?" But the rock wouldn't stop shaking.

"Hey, it's okay," she said. But something told her it wasn't.

She carefully made her way to the top of the hill and looked down the other side. Her heart thudded.

Below lay a wide, deep valley, covered in shifting mists. And through the flowing mist, Adriane caught glimpses of the valley floor. Deep gashes ran like open wounds ripped through the earth. They glowed with a sickly green. Black Fire.

"Oh, no!" Adriane gasped. The green glowed menacingly, moving in rivers through the valley, reaching for the mountains beyond.

She had seen the poison in the animals at Ravenswood. She had seen it dripping like venom from the manticore, but nothing could have prepared her for the magnitude of what lay before her.

Fear crept up her back. Nothing could survive the onslaught of such horrendous evil. She looked out at the mountains beyond. She had to cross this valley. They would have to skirt around the green rivers of poison.

She took a deep breath. "Come on. This way."

Mist crept down over the hillside. The rock took a tentative roll beside her, and stopped again. Adriane looked over and saw large shapes partially hidden in the fog. When they didn't move, she stepped closer. The shapes lay spread out upon the sloping hillside. She gingerly stepped closer and the mist parted to reveal bodies.

Adriane cried out, her hand covering her mouth.

They were huge animals. They reminded her of the wooly mammoths she had seen on a Discovery Channel special. What once had been an entire herd now lay still in the field. They were dead, all of them, covered in glowing green poison, horribly burned by the Black Fire.

Adriane fought back nausea. Tears ran down her face as she walked by the silent graveyard. The rock rolled right at her heels, not leaving her side.

What kind of world is this that would let such magnificent animals be slaughtered?

"Come on, Rocky, there's nothing we can do for them."

Adriane led the rock past the horrendous scene and entered the valley below, keeping a sharp eye out for the rivers of green poison. The air seemed to crackle with unsettling electricity. More and more, she felt as if she were being watched. She looked at the surrounding hills. Through the mist, she caught sight of something moving in the grass down the hill right toward them. Blue sparks of light flashed as it moved. And it was fast. Suddenly she saw more moving through the grass and down the hill to her left. She turned to look at the other side and saw dozens more racing toward them. Arcing blue flashes of electricity ignited sparks in the air as they moved.

Her wolf stone was pulsing with deep orange light.

"Rocky, we have to run!"

Adriane took off, her legs making long strides across the valley floor. Rocky rolled behind her, trying to keep up. She risked a glance over her shoulder and saw her pursuers moving faster.

Whatever they were, they were small—small enough to be hidden in the tall grass.

She didn't like this at all. She had to be careful not to run into the deep gashes of poison. And the flowing mist was making it very difficult to see.

She turned back and peered into the fog. Something screamed and lunged straight for her. She had a split second to register that it was jet-black with blazing red eyes before it knocked into her, sending her flying. Twisting as she fell, she folded her body into a tuck and rolled back up into a fighting stance. But there was nothing there. Whatever it was had vanished back into the mist.

More high-pitched screams erupted around her, surrounding her.

"Rocky? Where are you?"

Sharp pain lanced into her neck as something jumped her from behind. She screamed and whipped around, tossing the creature to the ground. The thing was instantly back on its feet. It looked like an inkblot in the shape of a small man with bright red eyes. A spark of electrical energy raced through its body with a snap.

It attacked again. This time, Adriane swung her arm,

and a blazing stream of fire whipped from her jewel. She turned, stepped to the side, and swept the fire upward, smacking the creature back into the mist. Four more came at her. Incredibly fast, they were on her before she knew it. Two went for her legs as the other two leaped for her head. Adriane jumped and kicked, knocking the lower ones against one another. She spun in a circle to shield her head as the other two screeched wildly, grabbing for her hair and eyes. Adriane screamed as magic fire exploded from her gem. Black ink splattered as the two creatures were ripped to pieces. Droplets rained to the ground, sparking and pulsing. Adriane watched in horror as the drops of black slowly moved together and rose up. The creatures began to re-form.

She dropped down, swiping her hair off her face, frantically searching for Rocky as she waited for the next attack.

To her right, the mist parted, and she saw a dozen of the inky things circling the rock, trying to keep it penned in the middle. Silver-blue sparks of electricity shot through the rock as they tried to trap it. She swung her arm, whipping out a long trail of magic and let it fly. Golden fire crashed into the creatures, splattering them into pools of black.

"Rocky! Over here!"

Before the things could re-form, the rock dashed past them to Adriane's side.

"Run!" she screamed.

They took off across the valley, streaking headlong

into mist—and stopped short. Across their path lay a glowing gash of Black Fire. It was too wide to jump.

Breathing hard, Adriane whirled around. The monsters had regrouped. Dozens were running toward them, screeching like mad spirits out of a nightmare.

Adriane looked back at the river of poison. It stretched into the distance both right and left. There was no way to run around it. They were trapped. The creatures were closing in fast. Rocky suddenly took off, rolling right at them.

"No! Rocky!"

The rock rolled into them like a bowling ball. The inky monsters went flying.

There was a rush of air, and dust and dirt swirled around her. Adriane fell to her knees, covering her eyes and mouth to keep from choking. Through her fingers, she saw a winged creature hovering above her. It had the body of a lion and the head of a giant bird. Its wings were enormous, spanning a good twelve feet. A hand suddenly reached down and grabbed her arm, pulling her up and tossing her onto the flying creature's back. Someone was sitting in front of her.

"I hate imps," the figure said simply, turning around to look at Adriane. Her jaw dropped. Adriane was pretty sure it was a human boy.

"Hang on!" he shouted, turning back to spur his mount. The creature's wings flapped and it rose into the air. Adriane twisted around to see Rocky still on the ground, toppling over as it desperately tried to jump.

"No! Wait! Let me go!" Adriane screamed. She bucked and struggled.

"Stop that! What are you doing?" the boy yelled, reaching back to try and keep her seated.

"Let me go!"

With a fierce push, Adriane flung herself off the flying creature. Grabbing its leg, she hung on, sending it careening into a dizzying spin. The surprised beast gave a loud squawk as it tried to shake loose its swinging baggage. Adriane hung on, forcing it toward the ground. Letting go, she dropped. She landed, rolled and sprang back up to her feet.

"Rocky!" she yelled.

The rock quickly rolled over to her and she bent to lift it. It was heavy! Adriane didn't know what to do. The imps were going to be on them in seconds.

"Hurry, pass it here!"

The boy was leaning over the side of the flying creature as it beat its powerful wings to stay in the air. She had no choice. She lugged the rock up to the boy, grabbed his other arm, and swung back up behind him. The imps swarmed, climbing on top of one another, madly grabbing at the flying creature's legs, igniting a flurry of sparks. The flying beast lashed out with sharp claws, splattering and toppling the pile of imps. Adriane hung on for her life as the mighty winged creature swept up into the sky.

7

ADRIANE WIPED HER eyes, coughing from the dust and grime. The valley below was a speeding blur of greens and browns. Ahead lay the mountains, their base draped in thick, swirling fog. The boy had wedged the rock securely between himself and Adriane.

She flinched as the boy reached down, retrieving something from an embroidered saddle bag. "Here, drink this." He handed her a soft pouch over his shoulder.

Very carefully, she let go of his waist with one hand and took the pouch. She flipped open the lid and took a careful sip. It was water. Warm, but it tasted clean and pure. She took long gulps. And she felt better.

"Thank you." She handed it back.

She studied the boy in front of her. He was maybe

fourteen or fifteen years old. His hair was sandy brown with blond streaks, long but not unkempt. His skin was bronzed, although Adriane saw no sun in the sky. He seemed healthy enough. He wore a loose-fitting white shirt with half the long sleeves ripped off, cloth pants stitched up the sides, and leather-like sandals.

"What kind of magic was that?" he asked.

"I've never seen creatures like those," Adriane replied.

The boy shook his head. "Not the imps, *your* magic."

She didn't know how much to tell this boy. "Uh . . . I have a gemstone. It controls magic, but I'm not very good at it."

"Not good?" The boy laughed. "You fought off two dozen imps!"

"You were watching me?"

"We've been watching you since you entered the valley."

"Nice timing," Adriane grumbled.

"What were you doing down there?" he pressed.

"I . . . I got lost."

"Lost? Where were you going?"

"I need to get to those mountains. I . . . uh . . . I'm looking for . . . my friend."

The boy spun around to face her, folding his leg beneath him, perfectly balanced on the winged animal's back. Eyeing Adriane curiously, he poked at her cheek and tugged her hair.

"Ow! Quit it! That hurts!" She knocked his hand

away, then quickly gripped his arm, as she tilted out over the swiftly moving ground far below.

"Are you human?" he asked.

"You know, I might ask you the same thing," she answered, pulling away.

"Are you?" the boy asked again.

"Yes. What else would I be?"

The boy shrugged. "You use magic—you could be anything."

Adriane was starting to get a little annoyed.

"What's with the rock?" He gestured with his chin, letting his long hair fly over his face.

"What about it?" she asked stiffly.

"You risked your life for it. Magic?"

"I don't know. I think so . . ." She hugged the motionless, silent rock.

The boy looked at her sharply. "Where did you come from?"

"Over the rainbow," she answered.

"How old are you?"

"One hundred and fifty."

His eyes opened wide. That shut him up.

"Look, who are you?" she asked impatiently.

"My name is Zachariah—Zach. This is Wind Dancer. I'm human. He's a griffin."

The griffin snorted a hello.

"I'm Adriane. Thank you for rescuing us."

"What are you doing out in the Shadowlands?"

"What are *you* doing here?"

"That's a stupid question."

"*Your* questions are stupid. You'd think you never saw another human before."

"I haven't," he answered.

That shut her up. What was he talking about?

Wind Dancer turned his head to Zach and gave a few angry squawks.

The boy looked up with a quick glance. "Hang on, we've got company." He swung back into his riding position.

Adriane twisted around. Behind them she could make out about a dozen figures soaring through the air, coming at them fast.

"Your little magic show has attracted a lot of attention," Zach said.

"What are those?"

"Can't tell yet. Too big for gremlins, maybe gargoyles. Nasty things."

"Worse than a manticore?"

The boy stiffened. His eyes narrowed suspiciously. "What do you know about manticores?"

"Nothing really. I . . . my friends and I met one once." Should she trust this boy or not? He *had* saved her life. He sure didn't seem to trust her much.

"Must be some friends," he grunted.

"They're gaining on us," Adriane yelled, looking over her shoulder.

"We can't outrun them, so we'll have to lose them," Zach told her calmly. "Hold your legs tight against Windy. When we turn, lean into the wind with us, keep your weight centered and hang on. Got that?"

"I think so." She told herself not to look down as she tightened her grip on the boy's waist.

Zach patted the griffin's neck, then wrapped his fingers in the big ruff of lion's mane that grew along the neck below the eagle head. "Okay, Windy, let's go."

With a beat of his strong wings, the griffin angled off to the right and dove straight down. The ground twisted, careening by at a dizzying speed. Adriane saw something white flashing on the mountaintops. When the mountains turned upside down, she closed her eyes and hung on tight as Windy dropped like a cannonball into the thick fog at the base of the foothills.

But even with hardly any visibility, Windy flew fast and sure.

"Whatever you do, don't use your magic," Zach shouted over his shoulder.

"Why not?"

Howls pierced the mist, echoing off the cliff walls behind them.

"They're magic trackers. Duck!"

Adriane obeyed—a second before a jagged rock flew just inches above her head. They were flying perilously close to the sheer cliff face. "Next time can I have *two* seconds?"

"Okay . . . duck!"

Windy dove under a wide arch that bridged a gap between mountains. They were flying through a narrow gorge, surrounded on both sides by long spikes of rocks that jutted out like rows of gigantic teeth.

Adriane looked down at a sheer drop into nothingness.

Windy gave a hissing snort.

"Are you using magic?" Zach accused.

"No!"

"They're still on us."

Windy gave the boy a few squawks. Zach was thinking, trying to make a decision.

"Windy thinks you're okay," he said finally. "Animals have a strong intuition."

"I wouldn't know," Adriane replied bitterly, thinking of Storm.

"We're going inside."

"How can Windy see anything through this mist?" she yelled.

"He knows these mountains cold." Zach laughed. The boy was actually enjoying himself. "Windy could find a craven's nest in an ice storm."

"I'll remember that the next time I need a craven."

"Besides, we've flown the Serpent's Teeth before . . . just never in the mist."

Windy dove and twisted, narrowly avoiding the spires and spikes that seemed to loom out of nowhere before disappearing back into the mist. Whatever creatures were trailing them weren't faring as well. Tremendous crashes were followed by painful howls that echoed over the gorges.

"Ooo, I bet that hurt." Zach chuckled.

Windy squawked, banked to the left, and flew straight for the mountainside.

"Where are we going?" Adriane asked, eyes wide.

"In there." Zach pointed directly ahead to the sheer rock cliff.

At the last minute, Adriane made out a thin vertical break in the cliff wall. Windy turned on his wing tip and slipped through the crevice. Adriane hung on tight and closed her eyes. They broke through the cliff wall, emerging into a wide canyon completely surrounded by mountains. The griffin straightened out and glided, perfectly balanced atop swift currents of cool air.

"Ha! Let those demons try *that!*" the boy whooped, hugging the griffin. "Good flying, Windy!"

The griffin spat back a response, reminding them how he felt about demons.

Adriane felt a pang of jealousy, thinking of the close moments she'd shared with Stormbringer. If Zach felt that way about Windy, he couldn't be so bad, could he?

The mists vanished as the griffin descended in slow circles. Below was a wide plateau crisscrossed with gorges. On the far side, the mountains rose, towering against swirling purple skies.

They dropped into a deep gorge. Adriane made out a swift-moving river at the bottom. Spindly trees dotted the scrub grass and ran up a slope to a series of caves cut into the rock wall. The griffin landed on the far banks of the running waters.

The boy slid from Windy's back and leaped to the ground. "We can stay here until everything calms down."

Clutching Rocky in her arms, Adriane slid to the ground. Her legs felt like rubber, and she could barely stand up. She gently dropped the rock and it rolled over to the riverbank, coming to a stop, then sitting motionless and silent.

Zach gave Windy a firm pat. With a snort and a shake of his eagle head, the griffin took off into the air. Adriane watched him fly away. "Where's he going?"

"To hunt. Don't worry, he'll keep an eye out for trouble." The boy turned and began walking up the slope toward the caves.

"Where are you going?" Adriane called.

"I have some dried fruits in the cave." He pointed to the river. The water runs down from the mountains—it's fresh and clean."

Adriane watched him walk away. A real human boy in Aldenmor—the *only* human, according to him. It was amazing. Then again, being in a magical world was amazing. So far it had been one shock after another.

What was it about him that bothered her? Should she

trust him? He seemed friendly, but there was something
. . . secretive about him that made her feel uncertain.

She plopped down on the bank of the river. Light
seemed to reflect evenly off the canyon walls although
there was no direct sunlight. She could have been sitting
at the bottom of the Grand Canyon, except that the rock
strata were layered with pastel green and orange instead
of the rusty sand colors of Arizona.

Adriane untied her hiking boots, took them off along
with her socks, and put her feet in the water. It was cold
and *sooo* refreshing. She bent over and splashed some on
her face and neck. Then she checked the rock.

"Having a good time?" she asked.

Leaning over, she rolled the large rock toward her feet.
"You need a bath."

Adriane splashed water over its crusted surface, peel-
ing away layers of mud and dirt. She was a bit surprised
at how much had built up. She stopped and inspected it.
A patch of yellow had appeared under the layers of
grime. Blue speckles seemed to shift against the yellow.
"Wow! Are you an ugly duckling?" She started scrubbing
harder and more layers of dirt and mud fell away.
Adriane's eyes widened. "Look at you."

Underneath the muck, the rock was shiny smooth, its
surface a pretty yellow, dotted with purple, blue, and
orange speckles. The colors were moving, melting in and
out of one another, reminding her of a mood ring.

"You are the most beautiful rock I have ever seen!" Adriane announced.

The rock beamed as the shifting colors shone even more brilliantly.

"That's not a rock."

Zach was standing behind her. He handed her a small slab of granite, a plate filled with dried apples, dates, and raisins. Adriane's mouth started to water.

"Go ahead. It's not poison." Zach popped a date into his mouth to demonstrate.

Adriane practically grabbed the slab away from him. She had never been so hungry in her life! "Thank you," she said, stuffing two dates into her mouth. Not bad, she thought, although right about now even a craven would taste good.

Zach was inspecting the now-clean rock, carefully touching it here and there with long, sure fingers. Looking worried, he bent over and put his ear to it. Then he pushed sandy hair from his face, and focused intense green eyes on Adriane. "It's an egg."

Adriane stopped in mid-chew. An egg? "How do you know—sorry." She finished chewing and swallowed. "I've never seen an egg like that."

"See this section?" He pointed to a shifting splotch of blues. She bent over to look, self-consciously aware of how close her face was to Zach's.

"The shell is thinner there," he explained. "And

warmer. Whatever's in there, it's alive, applying constant pressure to the weaker sections of shell."

Adriane sat back. *Alive!* It wasn't a rock after all. But then . . . what kind of egg was it?

"What do we do? Sit on it?" She smiled at her joke.

Zach broke out laughing. "No, I don't think it's a chicken." He fell over backward, holding his sides. Adriane laughed along with him—mostly out of relief that she was still alive.

"Nothing we can do." Zach chuckled, wiping a tear from his eye. "These kinds of eggs hatch when they're ready."

"These kinds?"

"Magic," the boy replied matter-of-factly.

Adriane tried to figure him out. It was time for some answers.

"What are you doing here—I mean here in Aldenmor?" she asked.

"I told you, I live—"

"But how did you *get* here? Did you fall through a portal also?" Adriane was suddenly terrified that if he did, he'd never found a way back.

"I was born here."

"Where are your parents?"

"Dead."

"Oh . . . I'm sorry . . ."

"I don't remember them," Zach explained. "They died when I was really little."

"How did you manage? I mean, how did you—"

"I was raised by . . . um . . ." The boy turned away. " . . . animals."

Adriane's eyes opened wide. "And you've never seen another human?"

"There are no other humans in this world, that I know of."

Adriane suddenly felt awkward. She didn't exactly consider herself the finest example of human society to meet the only boy from another world.

"I'm going to find Windy." Zach got to his feet.

"Then what?"

"I'll take you to the mountains. You said you had a friend there," Zach reminded her.

"Yes . . . I'm not sure where she is, exactly."

"The sooner you find a way to get home the better."

She looked at him uncertainly.

"This is a dangerous place," he explained.

"Oh, really. I hadn't noticed."

Zach's eyes twinkled and he smiled.

Adriane's eyes were downcast, but she smiled as well. "What do we do with our egg?"

Zach shrugged. "It likes you. Take it with you."

Great, a pet whatsit! That's all she needed. She slipped into her socks and laced up her boots, watching Zach deftly climb the steep slope above the cave opening. How could a human boy, hardly older than she was, have survived on his own here for so long? What wasn't he telling her?

She stood up and stretched her legs, watching the river wind its way around a bend in the gorge. She had crossed the valley and had made it past the foothills. Was she close enough to reach Storm?

She held up her wolf stone and concentrated, picturing the silver mistwolf. She began to turn slowly, gazing into the golden center of her gem.

"Storm," she called out. "Where are you?"

The light around the canyon grew brighter, reflecting off the water, until it suddenly flared out, washing her entire field of vision in pure white. She closed her eyes and felt herself once again race through a tunnel. Images flickered at the edges of her sight. She opened her eyes and looked at the mistwolf pack.

"Storm, can you hear me?"

"Yes. I am here."

The voice in her mind startled her. "Are you all right?" She could hear the other wolves. They were agitated, angry.

"Yes. Stay strong, warrior."

"Stormbringer!" Moonshadow stood in front of Storm, snarling. Adriane watched him through Storm's eyes. The great black wolf held Adriane in his golden eyes. Was he looking at her, or at Storm—or both?

"Was it not bad enough that a human killed our pack mother? Your human will only put you in danger. The pack must be protected. There will be no contact with humans! Never again."

Adriane cringed. She would never do anything to put Storm in danger. She could feel Storm's despair. Her best friend was torn between her new wolf pack and the human with whom she'd bonded.

Fog quickly gathered at their feet, and rose until it obscured Adriane's view. The mistwolves vanished—and Adriane was thrown violently out of Storm's mind.

She blinked, watching the sparkling river cut its path through the base of the ancient gorge. A human had killed the pack mother. But the only other human here was Zach.

8

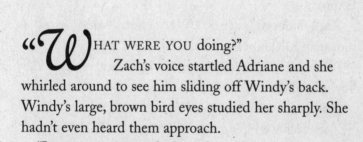

"**W**HAT WERE YOU doing?"

Zach's voice startled Adriane and she whirled around to see him sliding off Windy's back. Windy's large, brown bird eyes studied her sharply. She hadn't even heard them approach.

"I was . . . trying to find my friend," she said, covering the wolf stone with her hand.

"I told you not to use magic!"

Adriane felt her face redden. "It's not like there's no other magic in this world."

"This is not some game," Zach continued angrily. "You and your friends can't just show up here and start doing anything you want. Your actions have consequences."

"I know that." She crossed her arms defiantly. "But if my friend's in trouble, I have to help."

"The one in trouble right now is you. And us," he added, his gesture including the griffin, "now that we've helped you."

Adriane felt a stab of guilt. She didn't want them to get in trouble because of her.

Zach started pacing back and forth, brow furrowed. "Those creatures are not going to give up."

Pop!

"The last thing we need around here is more magic!"

Adriane looked around. That sound . . . it was so familiar.

Zach stopped pacing. "Who knows what horrible monsters will show up next!"

"Ooooo . . ." A red dragonfly head peeked over the boy's shoulder.

Adriane's eyes went wide.

Zach followed her gaze. "What the . . . !" He jumped back, swatting at the bat-sized dragon.

"Pweek!" The mini dragon leaped into the air, flapping shiny red wings, and hovered in front of Adriane.

"Fred!" she cried.

"Uh-uh . . ." The dragonfly shook its head.

"Uh . . . Barney?" Adriane guessed.

"Pweoooo!" the dragonfly said, angrily releasing a small spark.

"Fiona?"

"Deedee!" The red dragonfly landed happily on Adriane's shoulder, nuzzling her neck, her round jewel eyes sparkling.

Zach slapped his forehead. "What did I just say about magic?"

Pop! Pop! Pop! Pop!

Four more dragonflies, all different colors, popped in, chittering and flying around Adriane. She was never so happy to see anything in her life.

"Ooooo!" The dragonflies spotted the egg and zipped over, nudging one another aside for a chance to land on it.

"What are you doing here?" Adriane asked happily.

A yellow dragonfly—Goldie, she remembered— fluttered up to her, golden-faceted eyes twirling. Clearing her throat with a quick spark, she spoke carefully, "Kaaraa skeep a peep peep."

"What?"

Purple Barney jumped up, nudging Goldie away. "Keekee deedee!"

"What are they saying?" Adriane asked.

"How should I know?" Zach scanned the skies, as if a horde of monsters might drop in any second.

Windy stuck his head next to Adriane and let out a loud, deep squawk that startled everyone.

The little dragons screeched and hid behind Adriane. Fiona poked her nose up over Adriane's shoulder. "Poot!" she yelled back at Windy.

Windy turned to Zach and squawked again, a little more softly this time.

"Windy says they have a message from your friends at Ravenswood," Zach translated, checking out the blue dragonfly that had landed on his shoulder.

"What?" Adriane felt like dancing. "Well, why didn't you say so!"

The dragonflies all jumped back up and flew happily around Adriane.

"What's Ravenswood?" Zach asked her. "Is that where you live?"

"Yes. It's a wildlife preserve and my friends and I are guides there," she explained.

"I like the name."

The dragonflies all twirled and spun in a circle around Adriane. Fred dropped a small roll of paper into her hand.

"What's this?" She carefully unrolled the paper, turning it this way and that, studying the drawing scribbled on it. "Some kind of map?"

"Let me see that!" Zach grabbed the paper. As he examined it, his eyes narrowed.

"Where does it lead?" Adriane asked excitedly.

Zach looked up, astonished. "The Fairy Glen," he said as if he couldn't believe it.

"Yes!" Adriane almost jumped for joy. Ozzie must have drawn her a map and sent it with the dragonflies. "Why, that little ferret! The Fairimentals will help me find Storm!"

"Storm?"

"Um . . . the friend I'm looking for," she said, avoiding the boy's eyes.

Zach ripped the paper to shreds.

Adriane's hand flew to her mouth. "No, wait! What are you doing?"

"This must be destroyed."

"That was from my friends!" Adriane yelled. "It wasn't for you! You had no right!" Adriane felt like crying, but stopped.

Zach's face had gone ashen. "Who sent this?" he asked accusingly.

"Ozzie. He's an elf."

"An elf?"

"The Fairimentals sent him to Earth to find . . . humans," Adriane said.

"The Fairy Glen is the heart of this world!" Zach was clearly distressed. "What if the witch found this?" He threw the tiny scraps of paper into the river.

"You mean the Dark Sorceress?" asked Adriane.

Zach swung to face her. "She is using magic to destroy this world!"

Adriane's heart ached remembering the giant creatures lying dead across the hillside.

"First your stone, then these . . ." Zach started to say.

Fred sat on his arm and cocked his little blue head, smiling.

"Dragonflies," Adriane said.

"Yeah . . ." he went on. "She's probably got half the planet looking for us by now."

"Maybe that's the point," Adriane said slowly.

"You think she's after you?" Zach asked.

"She wants magical animals."

"Goook!" The dragonflies leaped into the air, bumped into one another, and popped out.

"Well, I think we can rule them out," Zach said. "And it's not Windy. There's no other magical anim—" He stopped.

The egg! It was sitting still, colors shifting boldly across its surface.

"She's after the egg!" Adriane concluded.

"Yeah, whatever it is, it's magical, all right. Windy even sensed it. I thought it was *your* magic attracting all the attention. It's that egg."

Zach stood still, as if he were listening hard to something. Ominous shadows moved slowly across the river as the sky darkened.

The griffin had stood up, his sharp bird eyes scanning the skies.

"What is it?" Adriane asked nervously. Something didn't feel right. She checked her wrist. Her stone was pulsing with bursts of amber light.

The griffin spread his wings, squawking and spitting loudly.

Adriane didn't have to ask what the spitting sound meant.

"We have to get out here . . . fast!" Zach leaped onto Windy's back.

Something streaked across the sky, smacked into the canyon wall with a *boom,* and ricocheted off like a flaming pinball. A tree exploded in flames, sending shards of wood flying everywhere.

Adriane ducked in terror, covering her head. Fireballs began to rain down into the canyon.

The griffin screeched up at the skies.

"Let's go!" Zach yelled at her.

Adriane skidded over to the egg, grabbed it, and hoisted it up to Zach. He stared at it for a moment, then took it, and reached for Adriane. Gripping his hand, she threw her leg over the back of the griffin and pulled herself up behind Zach.

Explosions rocked the riverbank as fire rained around them.

With a ferocious beat of his wings, the griffin was off the ground, Adriane barely holding on. Windy rose into the sky and stopped, hovering in place.

A dozen winged creatures had swarmed into a line across the top of the gorge, blocking their escape.

"Gargoyles!" Zach breathed.

Adriane could make out what at first looked like big, hairy, flying apes. Then she saw pointed leathery wings flap in the air, and wicked-looking bony horns that ran down their arms, backs, and legs. She could see their fierce, blazing eyes bearing down on them.

Windy circled. There was no way out.

The monsters advanced, flying slowly into the gorge.

Zach was desperately searching for an alternate escape route. "We can't get through them!"

A booming voice cut through the air. It was loud and gravelly and completely undecipherable.

Windy squawked.

Zach told Adriane, "You were right. They want the egg. They want us to hand it over and they'll let us pass."

Adriane hugged the egg close. "This is your world. What do you want to do?"

The boy sighed. "I'm open to suggestions."

Adriane scanned the ridgeline along the top of the gorge. She saw boulders balanced precariously along the edges. "Take us close to that wall," she said, pointing to the far side of the canyon.

"We'll be trapped over there!"

"I'm going to try and loosen those rocks on the ledge above," she told him.

"With what?"

"With this," she said, raising her wrist. The wolf stone pulsed with power. "If we can break their line, Windy can fly through the opening and we run like lightning."

"That's crazy!" Zach exclaimed.

"That's my suggestion."

The boy looked at the egg for a moment, then looked back at Windy. The griffin snorted his vote.

"Okay, let's do it."

Zach guided Windy toward the far wall of the canyon. The strata reminded Adriane of sand sculptures, layered with pastel shades of green, red, and purple.

Adriane scanned the ridgeline. Huge boulders lined the lip, hanging over the drop. Remembering how she had used the power of her stone to move objects before, she focused on the largest of the rocks. In her mind, she saw it moving, breaking free of its ancient bed.

The gargoyles had turned their line toward them, advancing like flying nightmares. Green fire sizzled between them, forming into a fireball that danced over their heads.

Adriane concentrated harder and felt a familiar sensation, like she was pushing through water. But it was too thick, too hard to break through. A drop of sweat ran down her nose.

Zach glanced at her and up at the rocks above them. "Go for the small one." He pointed to a spot below the boulder. "See? It's wedged just under the cliff line."

Adriane switched her focus to concentrate on the smaller rock . . . the water barrier felt thinner, and she pushed harder. The rock began to shake.

One gargoyle had flown forward in front of the others.

The green fireball flew across them and landed in the leader's claws.

"Hurry!" Zach yelled.

With a grunt, Adriane felt herself break through—and the rock came free, tumbling out over the gorge. It landed on the head of the lead gargoyle—and bounced off harmlessly.

Zach's face fell and his shoulders slumped.

The gargoyles closed in, making harsh guttural sounds. They were laughing. They knew their prey was trapped.

A sudden, sharp grating sound echoed above them, stone against stone. Thunder reverberated across the canyon as the entire ridgeline crumbled, sending truck-sized boulders falling into the gorge. Before the gargoyles could react, their line was torn apart, crushed by the impact of the two-ton rocks. The six in the middle were swept away and vanished instantly. The others chaotically scattered in surprise. The fireball exploded, sending the leader and two others smashing into the canyon walls.

With a fierce yell, Zach spurred Windy forward. The griffin didn't need any encouragement. He reared up and shot between the gargoyles, straight toward the top of the gorge.

The monsters were confused long enough for the griffin to break what remained of their line. But the last four were quick. They fell on Windy, tearing at the griffin's wings with sharp claws. The griffin screeched in pain.

Adriane was suddenly surrounded by the beating of leathery wings. She tried to shield her face, but long, sharp claws grabbed at the egg, trying to pry it loose from her arms. She gasped as wings beat around her head. One monster was on Zach; another had a stranglehold on the griffin's neck, trying to drag him down. Adriane's stomach lurched as the canyon walls tilted, the ground far below sweeping past at impossible angles.

A glint of steel flashed through the air. The gargoyle on Zach fell away, howling, one wing sliced from its body.

Windy was struggling to stay airborne as the other gargoyles swarmed over his head, trying to avoid the killing wrath of the boy's sword.

Adriane kicked out, knocking the creatures away from her, and freeing her arm. Another dove at the egg, wrapping its claws around it. Blazing red eyes blinded her as razor teeth tried to snap at her neck. She screamed and golden fire exploded from her gemstone. The force threw the gargoyle off. The other swooped in and grabbed Adriane's arms, pinning her gem against her waist. She couldn't move her arm. She watched in horror as the monster unhinged its jaws, opening a mouth full of razor teeth. The creature leaned into her face— and suddenly its head was gone, removed from its body with one cleave of the boy's sword. The monster's body fell back, green gore spurting from its neck as it fell into the gorge.

The last monster came at them, flying in fast. With all of her might, Adriane swept her stone into an arc and whipped out a blaze of fire. The power smashed into the gargoyle, sending it careening into the canyon wall. With a shriek, it fell and vanished.

The griffin soared out of the canyon.

"You all right?" Zach called back.

Adriane was shaking so hard, she was sure she'd lose her grip. Yet, through her sweat and tears, she still clutched the egg, holding it tight.

Windy dove into open desert, gliding low and fast.

Adriane watched, as if in a dream, as Zach pulled a small container from the griffin's collar. He bit off the lid, and poured dark, thick liquid onto Windy's side. It was then that she saw deep gouges had been ripped through his flesh—leaving ragged green lines of glowing poison. Black Fire.

The griffin gave a violent squawk, sharp eyes now glazed with pain. The dark liquid covered the worst of the wounds.

"Is he okay?" Adriane asked worriedly.

"He's hurt bad. I have to get him down before the poison reaches his heart."

"I'm so sorry!" she cried out. "It's all my fault!"

"Stop it!" the boy yelled. "Pull yourself together! We would have all been killed if you hadn't done that trick!"

Adriane bent over the egg, sobbing, wishing Emily were here to heal the brave griffin.

They coasted over a stretch of wide-open desert pocked with huge craters like the surface of the moon. The mountains towered in front of them as Zach guided Windy toward a pass between two of the tallest peaks.

"I've never seen creatures attack like that!" Zach said. "Whatever this thing is, it's important enough to risk a full-scale war."

"What do we do now?" Adriane asked.

"We have no choice. We're going to the Fairy Glen."

"But you tore up the map. How are we supposed to find the Fairimentals now?"

"I know where they are."

Adriane's eyes widened. What was Zack leading her into? She had no choice now but to trust his judgment.

She hugged the egg close, feeling the pulse of the new life within as they flew deeper into a world Adriane never could have imagined.

9

*T*HE DESERT QUICKLY gave way to tree-covered
foothills. Ahead, rivers fueled by melting snow
flowed through a labyrinth of fjords that divided the
upper mountain range. They were soon flying over fast-
moving water, following rough, white-frothed rapids
through twisting and turning ravines.

The griffin dipped suddenly, then regained his balance, snorting and gasping for air. Holding tight to the
boy's shirt, Adriane looked at Windy's wounds. They
were bad. Glowing green pulsed along thin arteries, fan-
ning into the griffin's wings. Whatever the boy had
poured over them must only have dulled the pain.
Adriane knew the courageous creature would never give
up until his heart burst—and hers along with it.

Zach leaned low, calming the animal, whispering soothingly. Adriane couldn't hear what he was saying, but she could see his hand stroking Windy's neck.

"How much farther?" she asked worriedly.

The boy straightened up. "The Anvil's just up ahead. It's not an ideal entry, but it's fast."

They were flying low enough to feel the spray from the rapids tumbling and rolling beneath them. Adriane tried to release the tension in her shoulders and focused on the strange sword now sitting quietly in its leather sheath by the boy's side. The intricately carved hilt was set with small, shimmering stones.

"I've never seen a sword like that," she noted.

"It's an Elven spirit sword."

"Are you a warrior?"

"I fight when I need to."

Adriane shuddered. "I hate it here. So many awful things. How can you fight for this?"

"That's not what I fight for," he said quietly.

The roar of rumbling water suddenly filled her ears as they crested the edge of a tremendous gorge. Beneath them was a cavernous opening in the earth completely surrounded by colossal waterfalls. It looked as if the gigantic circle of thundering water served as a drain for the entire world. Adriane gasped. These were the most awesome waterfalls she had ever seen.

She knew now why this place was called the Anvil.

Water hammered ten stories down, crashing into an inferno of white mist far below.

Zach gently ran his hand over the griffin's neck. "Which one, Windy?"

The griffin nodded his eagle head toward the largest of the mighty falls.

"Hang on. This is going to get a little bumpy," Zach called back to Adriane.

"Where are we going?" Adriane screamed over the deafening noise.

"That one," he yelled, pointing straight ahead.

Rainbows arced in the air, sparkling off spray from the booming falls. Behind, thousands of tons of water plummeted straight down, crashing into the abyss.

"We're going around that?" Adriane cried in astonishment.

"No."

"Oh." She sighed with relief.

"We're going through it."

The griffin dove toward the center of the falls.

Before Adriane could question the sanity of this action, she was rocked violently forward as water thundered over them. For an instant, she felt the pounding pressure would pulverize them like tiny bugs. But nothing happened.

She slowly opened one eye. Then the other—and gasped. Below were forests. Dense verdant forests that stretched forever under a brilliant sun. There were no waterfalls, no mountains.

"What happened?" she asked, her heart beating wildly.

"We took a shortcut," he answered.

She looked down and her eyes opened wide at the sight of beautiful rolling hills and—farmlands? Villages? "You said there were no other people here!" she exclaimed.

"No other humans," Zach corrected. "We're over the Moorgroves, near Arapaho Wells. This is elf country."

"Elves?" Adriane repeated in amazement. Ozzie had always insisted he was really an elf trapped in a ferret's body, but the reality of it had never hit her—until now. There was a thriving civilization here, while death and horror threatened not a few moments away. Adriane shaded her eyes to block the sun, and saw mountains way off in the distance. She had no idea how far they had come.

"How did we get here?"

"Through a portal," Zach said. "Aldenmor is riddled with them, if you know where to look. Probably like your world. In ancient times, some connected the worlds."

"Some still do," she said.

They had left the populated area and were above forests so thick Adriane couldn't make out individual trees. Windy's breathing was labored, and he wobbled dangerously, trying to keep airborne.

"We have to get him help!" Adriane yelled.

Zach wiped sweat from his eyes as he peered down at the trees below. "There, Windy," he commanded, leaning over and pointing.

The griffin dove into green and everything went gray. They were in a blinding mist. Where had *that* come from? There had been no sign of it from above.

The jolt shook Adriane as Windy landed hard. Zach was off the griffin in a flash, checking his wounds.

Adriane slipped down to cool, moist earth and gently placed the egg on the ground. She recognized the place instantly. The magic glade at Ravenswood! She was home!

Then she realized that this was not the place she knew after all. It only looked like it. This glade was much larger. A deep-blue lake lay before her, its surface broken by sparkles of sunlight, twinkling like diamonds. Along the shoreline, willows swept delicate branches across the water. Tall trees surrounded the glade like a wall. And the meadows around them were filled with the rainbow flowers that had been brought to Earth by the great fairy creature, Phelonius.

"This is amazing!" She turned about in awe—and stopped, her breath catching in her throat.

Windy lay on the ground. He wasn't moving. Zach was kneeling quietly by his side, gently wiping dirt away from the griffin's eagle head. The creature's once sharp, clear bird eyes were closed and he wasn't breathing.

"Oh no!" Adriane cried out.

The boy looked up, his cheeks stained with tears. "He's gone."

"But these flowers have healing magic!" She swept her arm over the field of rainbow flowers. "They can help him!"

Zach shook his head. "It's too late. The strain to get us here was too much."

Adriane ran to the griffin, forcing her magic stone to pulse with healing light. "Please," she called in a hoarse whisper. "Emily, tell me what to do!"

But there was no answer. The griffin was gone and her wolf stone could not call on the power of Emily's healing jewel.

"No!" She fell to her knees, crying.

A sound like tinkling bells drifted over her. Then it became a voice. "We are sorry."

Adriane turned. A thin veil of mist lingered in the center of the lake, lit from behind by a single shaft of sunlight. She blinked. Through her tears, Adriane saw a girl standing about ten feet from shore—*on* the water. The figure was made of water, flowing blue and green, swirling up from the lake itself.

"The griffin was a brave warrior," the watery figure said. The clear, pure water caught glints of sunlight as if the magic within sparkled.

Dust and dirt swirled behind Adriane. She covered her eyes. When she opened them, another figure stood next to her. It looked like tumbleweed woven together with twigs and leaves. Small branches stuck out at weird angles. "Sometimes magic can bring great loss," the creature said in a rustling voice.

"Who are you?" Adriane asked, looking at the fantastical creatures.

"I am Gwigg, an Earth Fairimental," the pile of twigs said, bits of leaves flying off it.

"I am Marina, a Water Fairimental," the water girl said, gracefully gliding to the shore's edge.

"You have come a long way." A light, airy breeze brushed past Adriane. She caught the translucent shape of something moving, flowing and hovering near her. "I am Ambia, an Air Fairimental," the breezy shape said.

Zach stood up and approached the Fairimentals. "Windy died to get us here!" he yelled angrily. "Why couldn't you help him?"

"The spirit of the griffin has come back to the magic," Marina said, her voice like silky chimes.

"Spirits of the past will always guide us into our future," Ambia whispered like the wind.

"Why did Windy have to die?" Zach cried, wiping tears from his face.

"We will weep with you," the Fairimentals gently answered together, combining their voices into a melody that drifted into a breeze blowing across the Fairy Glen. The willows swayed, releasing hundreds of tiny flowers upon the crystal waters.

"It was my fault," Adriane said, looking down at her

boots, dark hair falling over her face. "If he and Zach hadn't rescued me, Windy would still be alive."

"Why did you send an elf to her planet?" Zach asked the Fairimentals, trying to make sense of what was happening.

"For her," Marina answered.

"What's so special about her?"

"We need human magic users," Gwigg rustled.

"*I'm* human. I—" Zach kicked at the dirt. "I could learn magic, too!"

Ambia hovered around the boy. Adriane could just make out her shimmering shape. With a soft breeze, the Air Fairimental dried the tears on Zach's face.

"There are many levels of magic," Ambia said, her translucent shape glittering in the light.

Marina's sparkling eyes focused on Adriane. "She has the ability to become a mage."

A mage? Ozzie had used that word. A mage was a human who used magic.

"Only through the bond with a magical animal can magic be mastered completely," Marina sparkled.

"And now my friend is gone." Zach's shoulders slumped.

"You have brought us the Drake," Gwigg said, his strange shape of twigs and leaves reforming as he spoke.

Adriane looked at the egg sitting silently by her feet. "The Drake?"

"If the sorceress had gotten the Drake, the balance of power would have shifted."

"The sorceress must be stopped," Marina's watery voice chimed.

"Aldenmor must be healed," Ambia whispered.

"What is . . . the Drake?" Adriane carefully asked.

"A dragon," Ambia breathed.

"A red crystal dragon," Marina added, magic sparkling through her watery shape. "They hatch once every thousand years."

"A *dragon?*" The boy looked horrified. "Windy died to bring a *dragon* here? They are vicious and horrible creatures!"

"The Drake is a very powerful creature. When dragons hatch, they imprint, bond deeply, with the first person they see. The sorceress intended the hatchling to imprint on her, giving her magic of unimaginable power." Gwigg shuddered, bits of sticks and dirt falling to the ground.

"That's why the sorceress wants magical animals?" Adriane asked.

"Yes."

"The unicorn would have fallen if not for the blazing star." Ambia swirled around Adriane.

Adriane thought of Kara. She'd give anything to see that bright smile right now, even though, only a day ago, she would have been happier to wipe it off that smug face. She felt a sharp sting of homesickness. She missed her friends. "Can you send me home?" she asked the Fairimentals.

"Yes."

Adriane's heart leaped.

"Your destiny is clear, Adriane," Marina said.

"How do you know me?"

"You wear the wolf stone. You have made it yours."

"Wolf stone? That's a wolf stone?" the boy asked.

"My friend . . . that I'm looking for, is not exactly human," Adriane said to him.

"What is she?" he asked, his hands balled into fists.

"A mistwolf."

Zach's ruddy complexion reddened and his eyes blazed with anger. "A mistwolf!" he spat and stalked away.

Adriane, confused and hurt, looked to the Fairimentals.

"Zachariah was raised by mistwolves." Ambia's voice blew like cool wind.

This time it was Adriane's turn to feel shock. Moonshadow had said a human had been responsible for killing the pack mother.

Adriane ran after the boy. The time had come for secrets to be revealed.

10

WILDFLOWERS SWIRLED AROUND Adriane as she walked down the lush path in pursuit of Zach. Wide, lustrous leaves of purple, pink, and blue sprouted everywhere, lending the glade a gleam of rainbow brilliance. She wished she could explore this extraordinary place, and she had about a million questions for the Fairimentals. But she had to find Storm—and get home. Her Gran was used to her going off on her own, but she would certainly worry before too, long. Hopefully, Emily and Kara were covering for her.

The path led to a grassy meadow. In the center stood an enormous tree, giant branches stretching out in all directions from a trunk as thick as a house. In fact, it *was* a house—a tree house. Wooden platforms were cleverly hidden amidst the green boughs. They were connected by natural stairways made of branches and covered by foliage thick enough to keep out any rain or cold—although she wondered if there was really ever any bad weather here.

Zach was sitting on a platform two levels up, gazing out over the Fairy Glen.

"Hi," Adriane said shyly as she approached.

The boy remained silent.

"Can I come up and sit with you a while?"

"Suit yourself."

Adriane climbed up to join him. The platform formed the floor of a large room. Branches had grown around and through the floor, forming tree chairs and even a tree bed, with a mattress piled thick with soft leaves. Thinner branches hung down the sides, like green curtains.

"This is an amazing tree!" she exclaimed.

"This is Okawa," he told her.

She looked around. She didn't see anyone.

She pointed to the tree questioningly. Zach nodded.

She studied the enormous tree. Gran had always spoken about nature spirits but Adriane refused to believe her, shrugging it off as just plain weird. Yet this tree was very much alive. She could feel it.

Adriane politely bowed. "Hello, Okawa. I am honored to meet you."

The great tree rustled, and a few of the smaller branches seemed to bend in toward Adriane, enfolding her in the fresh green scent of leaves.

"He likes you," the boy observed.

"I like him, too." Adriane sat next to Zach and looked out at the lake. "I feel so protected here, so safe."

He cracked open a hard-shelled fruit that looked like a small red coconut and handed her half. "Okawa has taken care of me for a long time."

Adriane took the shell and drank the milky liquid inside. It was sweet and delicious.

"Thank you," she said.

"You can also eat the stuff inside, it's good."

As they ate, Adriane noticed an old steamer trunk next to them. It was open and she could see clothes, some old books, a spyglass, and a few assorted tools.

"What's all this?" she asked, pointing to the trunk.

"It belonged to my parents."

She reached in and picked up a photograph set in a brass frame. Two smiling, proud parents holding a laughing baby in their arms looked out at her.

"That's me," Zach said.

"The baby, I take it." She smiled.

The corner of Zach's mouth twitched slightly upward.

Adriane noticed an old pocket watch. "May I?"

He nodded.

She examined the watch. It was engraved in script lettering: "To Alexander, always yours, Graziela."

"A gift to my father from my mother," he explained.

"It's beautiful." She put it down and studied the boy. "How old are you, Zach?"

"I don't know."

"When was your last birthday?"

"What do you mean?"

"You know, birthdays . . . with birthday parties?"

Zach looked puzzled.

"You've never had a birthday party?"

"No."

"Well, it's fun. You wear silly hats and your friends give you gifts."

"My friend is dead."

"I'm really sorry . . ." Adriane felt her eyes brim with tears and quickly wiped them away.

"It wasn't your fault," Zach said.

They sat watching the sunlight play across the lake.

"Zach . . . tell me about the mistwolves."

"No!" Anger raged, threatening to boil over within the boy. He jumped up and walked away.

"Please, Zach. My friend is still alive. Won't you help me find her?"

Zach walked to Okawa's massive trunk, reaching for its strength.

"My parents were magic users," he said into the tree.

Adriane's eyes opened wide.

"They were killed when I was a baby. I was found by the mistwolves." He turned around, leaning his back against Okawa. "The pack mother, Silver Eyes, took me in and raised me. She taught me to run with the pack and to sing the wolfsong . . ." His eyes were dark with

sadness. "She loved me, and I loved her like my mother."

Adriane sat quietly, hardly breathing.

"I was the runt and my pack brother did not trust me. Now he is the pack leader."

Adriane flashed on the black wolf that had taken Storm . . . Moonshadow.

"A witch had begun using magic in terrible ways. We knew she was once human. Moonshadow believed humans did nothing but bring sadness and destruction. He thought I would bring ruin and death to the pack . . . and one day I did."

He slid to the floor, knees raised to cover his face.

"More than anything, I wanted to find the monster that had killed my human parents. I became obsessed with hunting it down. I thought that if I could prove my courage, Moonshadow would accept me in the pack . . ." He paused to steady his breathing.

"I was hunting in the Shadowlands with several of the pack when I found the creature. I was so full of hate, I thought of nothing for my packmates. Instead of avenging my parents, I . . . I led the wolves into a trap . . ." He faltered.

"What happened to them?" Adriane asked after a few seconds.

"I was the only one who escaped." The boy buried his head in his knees.

"One of the fallen wolves was Silver Eyes . . . my wolf mother."

Adriane sat quietly.

Zach took a deep breath, calming himself. "Moon-shadow sent me away. He said I would never be a wolf brother. I wandered for a long time until I met the elves. They took me in and fed me and brought me here, to the Fairimentals. I began my work for them, scouting, acting as their eyes and ears. When I found Windy, he was just a pup, caught in a trap. His parents had been killed, also. We've been together ever since . . . until today."

Adriane slowly rocked back and forth, hugging herself. "I never see my parents," she told Zach. "They might as well be dead. If it wasn't for Storm, I don't know what I'd do. And now, she's gone. She left me to run with the pack."

The boy sat watching her. "So we're both alone," he finally said.

"What's happened here, Zach? To Aldenmor."

"There was some kind of explosion in the Shadowlands. Since then the Black Fire has been spreading." He rose suddenly and walked to the edge of the platform, gazing out over the Fairy Glen. "Everything's changing so fast. Aldenmor is in terrible danger."

"Those poor animals I saw in the valley," Adriane whispered.

"Wilderbeasts. They once roamed all over that area, herds of them. Not anymore. And more animals are going to die if she is not stopped." His eyes blazed. "That is what I fight for."

Adriane stood up and joined him. "The Fairimentals must be proud of you."

"No. That's why they need you." He looked down. "I'm not good with magic."

"People have different ways of using magic," Adriane said. "My friend Kara, back on Earth, she doesn't have a gemstone, and she makes all kinds of magic just by being who she is—our magic just works better when she's around."

Zach listened intently.

"The way the Fairimentals treat you, the way Okawa cares for you . . . the way the Elven sword comes to life in your hands. Zach, everything about you is magic."

"No. You heard the Fairimentals. *You* have the gift, not me."

"Zach," Adriane said, searching his eyes. "I saw the way you were with Windy. You loved him. As much as I love Storm. I may not know much, but I have learned this: magic always starts here." She placed her hand on the boy's heart.

He looked at her hand, then into her eyes.

"I'm so sorry Windy is gone," Adriane continued. "But you have to go on. The Fairimentals need you . . . I need you."

"You . . . do?" he asked, eyes wide.

Adriane looked away. "You're everything I've always

dreamed of being. Strong, confident, independent." She turned to him again. "And you understand what's going on around here. How are we supposed to figure this all out without your help?"

"I'm not going back to the mistwolves."

"But it wasn't your fault. It was a horrible accident."

"You don't know that!"

Adriane took his hands in hers. "You could come back to Earth with me. You'd meet lots of friends and you could go to school and learn all kinds of things."

"You think I could fit in there?" he asked uncertainly.

Adriane smiled at him. "If I can, you sure can."

Zach didn't return the smile. He dropped her hand, turned, and walked to the branch stairway. "I'm going to take care of Wind Dancer."

"Can I help?"

"No," he answered sharply, then his voice softened. "I want to say good-bye alone."

Adriane understood and respected his wish. She watched as he started down. "Zach," she called after him.

He stopped.

"I'm going to find Storm."

"I know," he said, and walked away.

∞

THE BRIGHT SPECKLED egg sat on the sandy shores patiently waiting as Adriane walked back to the lake.

Colors swirled through the shell as she approached. She knelt down and patted it.

"It's time for me to go," she explained.

The egg quivered slightly.

"You have to stay here. The Fairimentals will take care of you now."

Deep blues and purples moved across the shell as the egg learned into Adriane's arms.

"C'mon, now don't get like that. You're going to make me all sad again." But she was already crying. She hugged the egg. "Thank you, Drake," she said softly.

From the corner of her eye, she caught the flutter of air. She could just make out the hovering, translucent shape of Ambia.

"You have many questions," the Air Fairimental said.

"Was the wolf stone meant for me?" Adriane asked, sniffling as she got to her feet.

"Nothing that happens is truly random." Ambia's cool voice brushed against Adriane.

"Why did you choose me?" Adriane asked.

"You are a warrior."

"No, I'm not. I'm scared all the time," she said angrily. "What kind of warrior is that?"

"The heart of a warrior is not measured by how strong you fight." Marina rose in tinkling chimes out of the crystal blue waters. "It is your spirit that connects you to the magic."

"Why me? The magic . . . I mean, don't I get a choice?"

"Why did you come to Aldenmor?" Gwigg's scratchy voice asked from the ungainly mass of twigs and dirt nearby.

"To find Stormbringer," Adriane said quietly.

"That is a choice of the heart." Ambia smiled. "That is why you have been chosen to find Avalon."

Avalon. It always came back to that mysterious place of legendary magic.

"What is Avalon?" Adriane asked.

"Everything around you . . . the sky, the earth beneath your feet, the magic itself—all are the forces of nature, of life. All are connected to Avalon," Gwigg spoke. "We have called on you to help us find it. To make the magic new again."

"If *you* can't find it, how are we supposed to?" Adriane asked.

"We are elemental spirits of this world," Ambia said. "We are bound to Aldenmor."

Gwigg swept around Adriane. "Three will be tested," the rough voice said. "One will follow her heart. One will see in darkness. And one will change, utterly and completely. This is the Prophecy of Three."

Ambia swirled across the grass. "It will take three—a healer, a warrior, and a blazing star—to find Avalon and heal the sadness. Only after each has met their challenge will you be ready."

"I don't know how to help." Adriane hung her head. "You need a knight, a hero, like Zach."

"This is *your* journey, Adriane," Ambia told her. "Even if you do not know, you know what is right."

"I can't do it without Storm."

"The mistwolves must find their own destiny." Gwigg spun close to Adriane and stopped. The Fairimental parted a thicket of leaves. A small, shining orb dangling from a metallic chain glistened.

"Give this to Moonshadow," the Earth Fairimental said. "It is a gift to help the mistwolves find their way."

Adriane took the sparkling orb from Gwigg and slipped it in her vest pocket.

"You must continue your path and follow your heart." Ambia swirled around Adriane.

A flash of light caught her eye. It glowed between two giant trees that surrounded the glade.

The Fairimentals' voices all blended together in a strange but beautiful harmony. "The magic is with you, now and forever."

Adriane looked at the Fairy Glen. It was so beautiful, so peaceful. She wanted to just sit by the water and feel the magic of the Fairimentals wash over her. To answer all her questions. Instead, she turned and walked away, toward the twinkling light hovering gently between twin towering trees. Adriane felt her wrist for the wolf stone and summoned her courage. She stepped into the light . . . and vanished.

11

THE SUDDEN BRIGHTNESS of snow-capped peaks made her shield her eyes. Temporarily disoriented, Adriane stood still, trying to get her bearings. She was on a hilltop near the base of the upper mountain ranges. To her right, great peaks rose above. To her left was the plateau that led to the smaller ranges. She could see the crisscross of gorges that ran like a ragged patchwork. She wondered which gorge Windy had hidden them in, and felt a stab of loss for the magnificent griffin.

She looked behind her, where she'd just been, and saw nothing unusual. Not even mist. The Fairimentals would take no chances that anything uninvited might find a way into the Fairy Glen. There would be no evidence, no signs, no clues to follow.

She zipped up her vest as a cool wind sent a chill through her. She felt something in her pocket. Startled for a second, she took out the sparkling orb given to her by the Fairimentals. Tiny stars twinkled in the small ball. It looked like a smaller version of the fairy map given to Kara by Phel; the map the girls had lost to the dark witch's manticore. Was this the same thing? Maybe the mistwolves would know, if she could find them. She slipped the gift back into her pocket.

The landscape was sparsely scattered with rocks, wiry brush, and short, wind-twisted trees. Ahead lay hidden valleys, covered in shifting, thick fog. This was a harsh environment. Suddenly Adriane thought she might have been a bit hasty leaving the Fairy Glen so soon.

Stay focused, she reminded herself. If the Fairimentals sent her here, the mistwolves must be close by. She had no choice but to use the wolf stone to contact Storm. She would have to chance any magic trackers. She couldn't just wander around without some direction.

She held up her wrist and concentrated, forming an image of Storm in her mind. Immediately, the gemstone pulsed with golden light.

"Stormbringer," she called softly. "Where are you?"

Adriane stretched out, reaching harder.

The smell of earth filled her senses. Cool grass cushioned her feet. She felt dizzy suddenly as the landscape moved past her. Gray shapes came into focus in front of her eyes—in front of Storm's eyes.

"Storm!"

She was running up a hill with several other wolves.

"I am here."

Adriane's heart leaped at the sound of the familiar voice in her head. "Where are you?"

"The pack is on the move."

Through Storm's eyes, Adriane saw them. Several hundred mistwolves, adults and pups, cresting the hill before her. The smell of the pack filled her nose and she longed to run with them. Storm howled, and the pack howled in return. The wolfsong filled her heart. Adriane threw back her head and howled with them.

"Stormbringer!" a different wolf growled.

Moonshadow stood before her, eyes blazing. *"The human will not join the pack."*

"I have brought something for you from the Fairimentals," Adriane said eagerly.

"Is this some human trick?"

"She is my packmate," Storm growled as she faced the pack leader.

The wolves circled around Storm.

Adriane felt her own lips pull back into a snarl. She growled—or was it Storm?

"Human," Moonshadow said to her.

With a start, Adriane realized the pack leader was talking to her.

"We are moving, seeking a new pack home far away from here. The pack must be protected. We need Storm now."

"The Fairimentals want you to have this gift," Adriane said. "I think it might help you find your new home."

Moonshadow snarled. *"I will give you until the two moons rise in the sky to bring this gift to me. If you are not with us in that time, so be it."*

The wolves began to disappear into mist.

"Storm, how do I find you?" Adriane asked quickly.

"The magic is with you," Storm's voice echoed through the mist and disappeared.

Adriane blinked. Sparse, empty hills stood before her. The sensation of sharing the wolf's mind, of being a wolf, had filled her heart with joy. To be separated from that made her feel so empty. She shivered.

The pack was leaving, migrating to a place far away. She had until Aldenmor's two moons rose over the valley to find them. Reaching out, she spun slowly in a circle, silently calling Storm. When she faced the hills to her right, the wolf stone glowed. Dusting herself off, she headed down into a valley of shadows.

The valley was thick with trees. But these woods were not inviting like the lush forests of the Moorgroves. Here the trees seemed to twist and bend, fighting against one another, struggling for a foothold in the rocky earth.

She wound her way around giant, gnarled roots and misshapen logs until she came to a dirt path. The going was easier, with better visibility, so she could see if anything was coming—which also meant that whatever she saw could see her, too.

She tried not to think about that and focused instead on what she had learned from the Fairimentals.

Three will be tested. One will follow her heart, one will see in darkness, and one will change utterly and completely.

What did that mean? She wished Emily and Ozzie were here to help figure it out—they were much better with riddles.

Were they each being tested in some way? Emily had learned to be a healer and had healed the animals at Ravenswood. Kara had saved the unicorn. Now was it *her* turn?

Three will find Avalon and heal the sadness. Heal Aldenmor? She should have asked the Fairimentals more, but she had a feeling they didn't have all the answers either. What was happening on Aldenmor was only the tip of the iceberg. If this sorceress—this witch— was not stopped here, Aldenmor, Earth, and the web— even Avalon itself—would not be safe. What would happen then? She shuddered. She had spent most of her life learning to live with loneliness, but she had never felt more alone than she did right at this minute.

Crunch!

Adriane spun around, ready to defend herself.

Nothing.

A dry branch cracked nearby. Then another. Behind her. She turned, but saw only gnarled trees, thick with thorns.

Searching for a good place to hide, she spotted some

large rocks partway up the side of a gully. Rivulets of melted snow formed splotches of water, some running into small streams, some lying stagnant. She tried to avoid splashing in the puddles as she scrambled up the ravine and ducked behind the rocks.

She waited. Her heart was beating fast, and she took deep breaths, willing herself to calm down.

A loud snap behind her made her jump. Something was pushing through the dense undergrowth, coming right toward her. Adriane gasped, thinking of the small, agile imps. She looked left and right. She had made a strategic error. The rocks she thought would hide her were boxing her in.

Adriane stood, back to the rocks, and held her gemstone out before her, its golden light pulsing . . . and waited.

Nothing happened. Cautiously, she stepped forward and parted the thick brush, slowly opening the vines and bramble. There was something there all right—

"Ahhh!" Adriane fell backward as the big speckled egg, bright colors swirling happily, rolled out on top of her.

"What the . . . ?" she exclaimed.

The egg tilted over and lay on her.

Adriane sat up, cradling the egg in her lap. "What are you doing here? You're supposed to be back in the Fairy Glen! Bad egg!"

The egg's colors shifted to blues and purples, and it quivered. Adriane rolled it to the ground and got to her feet, shaking her finger. "Oh, no!" Don't give me that. You are a very bad egg!"

The egg shyly leaned into Adriane's legs, shaking.

Adriane looked down and sighed. "Okay, okay. I didn't mean it. You just surprised me." She knelt down and hugged the egg. "I'm glad to see you, too. I missed you."

The egg beamed with bright colors.

"Do the Fairimentals know you followed me? You know I'm going to have to take you back to the Fairy Glen—if I knew where that was. But I don't. So I guess you'll have to come with me to meet the mistwolves."

Bright colors swirled over the surface of the egg as it bounced up and down.

"But *then* I'm taking you back."

Adriane climbed down from the rocks and started on the dirt path again. The egg rolled after her.

"Say, you didn't happen to bring any of those red coconuts? No? Just wondering. And I like your name, Drake. It's so smooth, like a rock star." Adriane laughed. "Rock star, get it?"

The egg tagged along right by her side, glowing brightly.

"Never mind."

They continued across the valley floor. The trees began to thin out. The rivulets became streams, and the ground started becoming rockier. Several times Adriane had to help the Drake over fallen trees and jutting stones.

"Okay, let's take five," Adriane said as they came upon a deep gully. A small stream ran though it. She was thirsty, but she dared not drink the water, which might not be safe. She slid down the hill to the stream and sat down against a tree. The Drake rolled down and leaned into her.

"I wonder how much farther it is." She huddled close, arm around the Drake. "Looks like we're almost across the valley. I just need to rest for a bit . . ."

Something shook Adriane awake. She opened her eyes. How long had she been sleeping? The Drake sat silently shaking next to her, ribbons of bright red swirling. Adriane looked closer. Two reptilian eyes opened just under the surface of the shell.

Adriane gasped. Something tickled at her mind. She fell over as the ground trembled. What was that? She barely had time to look around before another shock wave hit, sending vibrations up and down her spine. Her wolf stone was pulsing with a strong, amber light. She recognized the pulse immediately as a signal of danger. She heard the sounds of monstrous feet slamming into the ground. Something was coming—something big!

12

ADRIANE PUSHED THE heavy egg up the sloping side of the ravine. It was fiery red and warm to the touch. She glanced over her shoulder. Whatever was coming was getting closer. If she had to fight it, she wanted the advantage of height.

"C'mon, Drake." She pushed the egg over the top of the slope as a tree fell over, smashing to the ground behind her.

Adriane whirled around and gasped.

It stood at least ten feet tall, massive with muscle. It had the head of a pig, with long curved teeth protruding from its bottom lip. Slightly hunched, its arms were like tree trunks. One giant hand held a double-headed ax, the other a gigantic round shield. Its beady, black eyes looked up at her and the egg. Its mouth turned in a vicious grin. The thing grunted something unintelligible and stepped forward, enormous feet with pointed claws hitting the ground, making it tremble.

Adriane scrambled over the top of the gully and stood protectively in front of the egg. She raised her gemstone, hoping it was powerful enough to stop this monster. The thing raised its ax. She braced herself as it stomped up the ravine.

Something flew through the air, swinging in on a vine—and crashed into the giant. Eyes widening in astonishment, the huge thing toppled over and fell back down. The ground shook as it hit bottom. Adriane carefully peered over the hillock—someone jumped up, knocking her back.

"Are you okay?" Zach looked down at her.

"No!" Adriane yelled. "What are you doing here?"

"Rescuing you." He grabbed her hand and hoisted her to her feet.

Adriane ran to the egg and struggled to lift it. "Nice of you to drop in."

"I thought so." He edged her aside and hefted the egg in his arms. Together, they took off, running along the ridgeline. Zach searched for a place to hide.

"Couldn't live without me, huh?" Adriane called after him.

"More like the Drake here couldn't live without you," Zach replied.

They leaped across a small chasm to a dusty ridge. The cliff wall below was filled with rounded caves.

"We'll have to borrow one of these caves. We can't fight them"

"Them? As in more than one?"

"They're in a patrol, six of them."

He placed the egg down and carefully leaned over to examine the caves.

"Six?!" One was horrible enough. "What are they?"

"Orcs. Disgusting." He spit on the ground, reminding Adriane of something Windy would have done. "We'll have to hide out and hope they pass us by."

"And if they don't?"

"Orcs aren't too bright. You'll think of something," Zach said.

"Thanks for the vote of confidence."

She watched Zach slide down the hill and begin sweeping branches and debris aside, uncovering a large opening in the ravine wall. His Elven sword was strapped to his back.

"This one looks empty," he announced. "Come on." He held out his arm and helped Adriane slide the egg into the hole. She followed, hoping they weren't disturbing anything too nasty inside.

It was dark and musty, but from the opening they could see all the way to the valley floor below. Adriane placed the Drake near the back of the cave while Zach quickly pulled back the brush and branches to cover the opening. They could just see through the debris, which acted like a screen.

Zach turned to Adriane. "Here." He took out three small red coconuts from his pocket.

Adriane smiled. "You came all the way here to bring me coconuts?"

"I thought you'd be hungry."

"Well, I am. Thank you." She put two in the deep vest pocket next to the orb, and cracked open the other, gratefully drinking the delicious milk inside.

"Actually, the Fairimentals sent me to bring back you-know-who." He gestured with his thumb and turned to look through the screen of brambles. "Orcs aren't great magic trackers but they can sense the Drake."

"What do we do if they come?" she asked.

"You'll have to create a distraction."

"Good idea. I'll just run around and they can chase me for a while."

"I was thinking of something a bit more magical," he said, looking at her wolf stone.

Adriane followed his eyes. "Oh. I can do that."

Zach crawled back to examine the egg. "What's with the Drake? It's all hot. I can barely touch it."

"I know. And it's all red."

The boy's eyes met hers. "I have to get it back before—" His face grew pale.

"Before what?"

Zach blinked. "You think those orcs are monsters? You

have no idea what a dragon is. It's mean, and vicious and, and—horrible!"

"How do you know that?"

"Because."

"Because why? Have you ever met a dragon before?"

"Well, no . . ."

Adriane crossed her arms. "So you're just assuming it's a horrible monster."

Zach turned away and crawled back to the opening. "Everyone knows it's true."

"Well, I don't. And no one is going to harm this egg!"

The ground outside trembled. The orcs were approaching.

Adriane tossed her empty coconut shell aside and kneeled next to the boy, peering out.

"They're coming this way," he said.

"I'm going to try something." She held up her stone and concentrated, focusing on the trees across the ravine. She pictured them shaking and rattling.

Suddenly orcs came into view, their ugly pig snouts opening and closing, drooling over fearsome boar's teeth. Some carried axes, some wielded spears.

Adriane concentrated harder and across the gully two trees shook. Maybe she could fool them by sending a ghost image of the egg and placing it behind the shaking trees.

The orc leader stopped and sniffed at the air. It looked at the far side of the gully and moved in the direction of the trees.

"It's working," Zach whispered. "As soon as they cross that stream, we'll make a break and run."

"Where?"

Zach looked at her. "I go back with the egg, and you . . . go where you have to."

"You could come with me," Adriane suggested.

"No way. Even if I wanted to, I couldn't bring the egg to the pack. Trackers would be all over them."

Adriane hadn't considered that. She could be putting the entire pack in danger by bringing the egg there. "But the Fairimentals want me to give this to Moonshadow." She held out the sparkling orb on its chain for Zach to see.

"They gave you that?" he breathed, eyes wide.

"Yes, what is it?"

"A fairy map," he told her.

So it *was* like the gift Phelonius had tried to give Kara. "What is a fairy map?"

"A map of portals."

"So the mistwolves can leave," Adriane realized sadly.

"So they can leave *safely*," he corrected. "Hey, don't forget your mistwolf abandoned you to fend for yourself here."

"What's that supposed to mean?" Adriane shot back in anger, slipping the orb back into her pocket. The pack might have treated Zach callously, but Storm would never treat Adriane that way! Would she?

"Just that the pack leader has his own agenda. And the pack will follow him."

"So you're saying Storm isn't coming back."

Zach's eyes filled with compassion. "I don't know, Adriane. Things change."

He turned to look back outside. "Get ready to move—they're across the stream.

"Be very quiet."

Craaack!

Adriane jumped. "What was that?"

"It wasn't me," Zach said.

"Well, it wasn't me, either."

A high-pitched screech filled the cave.

The orcs had stopped and were looking around suspiciously.

Adriane and Zach exchanged stares.

"If it wasn't me or you . . ." Zach began as they both turned to look behind them.

The egg had a big crack right down the center.

"Oh, no!" Zach scrambled over to check it out. The egg writhed suddenly, its sides splitting into a dozen smaller cracks. Zach watched in horror as shards of shell crumbled. A low whine began to emanate from within. The egg was starting to hatch!

The boy's eyes widened in terror. "Make it stop!"

"What?! Are you crazy?"

With a screech, a single hideous claw broke through the shell.

"We've got to get out of here!" Zach kicked away the brambles covering the cave opening.

Adriane had a sinking feeling that the Drake might not be what she expected. The creature inside the egg was screeching like a banshee. A second clawed foot kicked out another section of egg. Two red reptilian eyes opened and peered out at her. As Adriane stared into those eyes, something flashed in her mind.

Zach grabbed her shoulder, whirling her around. "Let's go! Now!"

Adriane didn't know what to do. What if whatever was hatching was worse than what was waiting outside? She was trapped between an egg and a hard place.

13

ADRIANE STUCK HER head out of the cave. The giant orcs were stomping across the gully . . . right toward them. She looked back at the hatching dragon egg. "What do we do?"

"We run!" Zach grabbed Adriane's hand and yanked her out through the opening. They skirted the top of the ravine, making for the next valley. Zach was determined to put as much distance as possible between themselves and whatever monsters were behind them.

Adriane couldn't get those eyes out of her head. It was as if the dragon were calling to her, connected to her.

"Wait!" she yelled, pulling Zach to a stop. "I can't leave

Drake. I'm going back!" Adriane whirled around and ran back atop the ridge.

"I was supposed to bring back an egg," Zach shouted after her. "Not a live dragon!"

Adriane leaped over the ridgeline, sliding and skidding down toward the cave.

Bent low, she scrambled inside. All that remained were goo-covered shell fragments. Whatever had hatched was gone.

Zach tentatively peeked into the cave. "Well?"

"It's not here!" Adriane shouted.

"Oh, great." Zach slumped, head in hands, trying to figure out what to do.

Adriane spotted something out of the corner of her eye. Something in a shell fragment. She bent, pulled it free, and looked at it. It was a stone—rough-hewn but definitely some kind of crystal.

"Come on, Adriane!" Zach yelled in to her.

She slipped the stone into her breast pocket and climbed outside. "Which way?" she asked.

The ominous booming sound of marching feet resounded from the gully below.

"Not that way," Zach said, pointing.

Adriane's breath caught in her throat. Six orcs crashed through the trees, grinding rocks and logs into dust under their heavy feet. They brandished mismatched, battle-worn swords, spears and shields, some chipped and stained from other bloody battles.

She heard a swish and caught sight of a glint of steel. Zach had drawn his sword. A hint of fire licked up and down the finely honed edges, as if it were hungry for battle.

Adriane frantically scanned the area for anything that might have just recently hatched.

Ching!

A giant spear appeared in the wall not a foot away, sending clods of dirt flying in all directions. Adriane jumped back in shock and felt the loose earth beneath her feet give way. She was slipping. "Zach!" she called, desperately scrabbling for a handhold.

He grabbed for her arm but the hillside slipped down into the ravine, Adriane along with it.

"Ahhgh!" She landed hard on the gully floor.

Six orcs crashed across the steam, barreling down on her. She jumped to her feet, raising her wrist. The magic flowed from the stone like amber fire, swirling up and around her arm.

The orcs grunted and slowed at the sight, obviously aware of magic fire.

Zach landed in front of her, sword raised and glowing with fierce power. "Go for their legs," he yelled over his shoulder. "The hamstring just behind the ankle!"

The orc leader snorted, long upturned teeth moving on both sides of its pig snout. Beady, black eyes filled with rage, it roared, lunging at them with battle-ax raised—and suddenly stopped. The others stumbled as they barreled into him. The orc leader held his thick arm out to the side, its beady eyes now full of total terror.

"That's right, we're bad!" Zach taunted.

Adriane watched in amazement as the orcs started to shuffle backward. Then, squealing like pigs, they broke rank and ran away.

"Ha! Guess we showed them!" Zach turned around with a grin . . . which suddenly twisted into a horrified grimace.

"What?" Adriane had only to look at the gaped-mouth expression on Zach's face to know that whatever had really scared those orcs away was standing right behind her.

"Maamaa!"

Adriane turned at the cry ringing through her mind. She had never seen anything like it. It was a dragon all right or at least what she thought a dragon looked like! It was about the size of a really big dog. It sat back on two large feet. A rounded belly tapered off to a thinner chest with two arms and a long neck. It was covered with smooth scales in a variety of red colors, ending with a long, wagging tail, shaped into an arrowhead at the end. Its two silky wings shifted in colors, just like when it was still in its shell. It had a spiky ruff at the neck, not unlike a lion's mane, and two stubby, rounded horns jutting out from behind oversized, pointy ears that bent over at their tips. It actually reminded Adriane of a big puppy. Its long horse-like face had a wide mouth filled with tiny, sharp baby teeth.

This was the fearsome monster that everyone was so worried about? It was just a baby and it was crying—

"Maamaa!"

—for its mama. Uh-oh.

"Maaaaaama!"

The dragon lumbered toward her, tripping over feet much too big for its body. Joyfully, it bumped against Adriane. She hugged it. "Steady there," she said with a smile. She looked at Zach. "Look, Daddy. Baby's taken his first steps."

Realizing his mouth was still hanging open, the boy closed it, put his sword away, and stomped over. "I'm taking *baby* back to the Fairimentals right now."

The dragon buried its head behind Adriane, sweeping its body around and knocking its big tail into the boy. Zach went flying into the stream.

Drake sniffled, resting his long snout on top of Adriane's head. She wasn't afraid at all. She felt a bond, familiar and strong.

"Aww, it's okay, little guy," she cooed, scratching him under his chin. "You scared away those mean old monsters, didn't you? Yes, you did."

Zach stammered, tried to speak, but spat out water instead.

"You hungry, Drake?" Adriane reached into her pocket

and pulled out a coconut. She cracked it open and held it up to the dragon's mouth.

Drake stuck his snout in the coconut and happily lapped up the milk with his forked tongue.

"There, good baby," she cooed.

Zach had begun to pace back and forth in the gully, arms waving. "This is just great!"

"What's with you?"

"I'll tell you what's with me. The dragon has imprinted on you! He'll never let me take him back now. And I can't take him to the mistwolves. You're going to have to come back with me to the Fairy Glen."

"I can't. I only have until the moons rise. I'll never get to Storm in time."

"Well, we can't sit here!" Zach turned to look downstream. "Those orcs are dumb, but once they realize it's a *baby* dragon, they'll be back. Then what do we do?"

"UrRRRrp!" Drake belched a small fireball.

"Ahhh!" Zach's butt was suddenly crisped with black soot. He jumped up and down rubbing his smoking rear and yelling, "You big dummy! I'm not an orc!"

Drake lowered his head, cowering behind Adriane, one wide eye watching the boy dance around.

"I told you! That thing is dangerous!" Zach yelled.

"He didn't mean it." Adriane scratched behind the dragon's ears. The scales were amazingly soft. "Shhh, it's okay. Good dragon."

Her face was suddenly covered in sloppy wet dragon licks. Adriane giggled.

Zach walked over, brushing off soot. "You're still gonna have to come back with me."

"Drake, now you have to listen to me," Adriane told the baby dragon.

Drake sat, panting like a big puppy.

"I can't take you with me. You have to go with Zach to the Fairy Glen. Do you understand?"

Drake cocked his head and eyed Zach.

Zach forced a big smile over his face.

"See? He's okay," Adriane said.

She started to walk away. "Good dragon. Now stay with Zach. Stay."

She had gone only a few yards when Drake leaped up and ran to her, big feet clomping in the dirt. *"Maamaa!"*

"No, no. You have to stay with Zach! Ohhh . . ."

Panting happily, Drake reached out and gave her a big hug, slobbering all over her head.

"Oh, it's no use," Zach said in dismay.

A terrifying roar split the air. Followed by the thundering boom of feet.

Zach turned, whipping his sword free from its sheath. "They're coming back."

"Let's get out of here!" Adriane yelled.

"Good idea."

They ran down the gully, following the stream. Zach

was out in front, and Drake clumped behind Adriane. The ravine was getting deeper and narrower. Soon this stream would be a river and Adriane knew where that would eventually empty out. They ducked under logs that had fallen over the ravine like bridges.

The sound of marching feet echoed behind them. Those orcs were persistent.

"Let's get out of this ravine!" Zach shouted.

The sides of the ravine now rose up into muddy hillocks. They started up, but Drake was having trouble climbing, his feet sliding back in the mud.

"Get Drake over that hill," Zach said. "I'll hold them off."

"Wait." Adriane held his arm. "You're stronger than I am. You push him up, I'll hold them off."

Zach bit his lower lip, and then agreed. "Okay. But as soon as we're over, you'd better be right behind us."

Adriane faced Drake, looking deep into the dragon's eyes. "Now you listen to me. You go with Zach. I'll be with you very soon."

The dragon seemed to sense what she was saying and allowed Zach to push him up the steep side of the ravine wall.

Adriane slid back to the flat ground. With a crash, the trees ripped away and the orcs broke into the gully. She was suddenly facing six giants armed with extremely unpleasant weapons.

She glanced over her shoulder and saw Zach shoving

Drake toward the top of the hill. The dragon's head was craning back on its sinewy neck trying to see her.

Turning back, she whirled her arm in a circle, releasing a wave of golden fire, spinning it out like a lasso. Crouched in a fighting stance, she braced herself for the attack. She didn't have to wait long.

The orc leader, this time ready for magic fire, raised its shield and lunged forward.

Adriane swirled the fire around her. She threw out her arms and released the ring, sending it spinning out like a huge flaming Frisbee. It slammed into the orc, but its shield fractured the magic, sending it sparking into the trees.

Whoosh!

Spears flew at her. She dove, tucking and rolling away. The spears flew past her as Adriane landed in the shallow water of the running stream.

The orcs were forcing her out into the open so they could surround her.

She heard a whine in her head. *"Maamaa!"*

Oh, no. She whirled around to see Drake leap from the hill. He opened his new wings, but they weren't strong enough to hold him. His belly smacked in the mud with a *thwack!*

The orcs stopped uncertainly.

Drake rose up on his hind legs and roared. A lick of flame escaped his lips.

The orcs backed away. The dragon took a step forward and promptly tripped over his feet, falling flat on his nose.

The orcs snorted with laughter and raced forward.

"No!" Adriane threw herself in front of the dragon, diving to the ground and firing a stream of magic. The fire whipped out and wrapped around the ankles of two orcs. Adriane rolled, sprang to her feet, pulling her fist down sharply. The fire tightened, and the orcs went down, thundering into the water. Adriane leaped away as an ax split the air, cleaving into a boulder, sending splinters of stone flying. She danced and twirled, her gemstone exploding into blinding light that crisscrossed around her, creating a shield. Shards of rock bounced away.

White-hot pain pounded into her shoulder and she flew across the gully, landing face first into the water. She got groggily to her feet, hair streaked and dripping. Drake lumbered over to her, shaking with fear. The orc that had hit her towered over them as the others advanced. There were too many.

The orc raised its ax and swiped—but only the wooden handle came down, plowing into the muddy bank. It watched in surprise as the blade went flying into the trees.

Zach was standing on a natural bridge formed by a dead tree that had fallen across the ravine. His sword was out and ready. The orc threw away the ax handle, roared, and reached out with enormous hands to crush Zach like a fly. But the boy was too quick. The stunned orc looked down at the sword plunged deep into its chest. Its rib

cage opened with one terrible swipe. The boy kicked the bewildered monster back, and it crashed into the others like dead weight.

"Grab my hand!" Zach screamed. He had shimmied down and stretched out to grab Adriane.

"Hurry!" Zach leaned over farther.

Adriane looked at the regrouping orcs and then at Drake. Zach could save only one of them.

She reached into her vest pocket and raised her arm.

Zach slid lower, grabbing at her hand. Adriane slid her hand into his, but instead of grabbing on, she slipped the chained orb into the surprised boy's outstretched fingers.

She looked into Zach's eyes. "Take the Drake," she said, and pushed the dragon's tail into the boy's hand.

A look of shock registered on Zach's face. But he pulled with all his strength and yanked the startled dragon up beside him on the tree bridge. Then he leaped to his feet and ran, pushing the crying dragon away from the ravine.

Adriane threw back her soaking hair and stood facing the orcs. On her wrist, the golden wolf stone pulsed like the heartbeat of a warrior.

"Is that the best you can do?" she yelled.

"Adriane!"

Adriane looked back and saw the boy standing next to Drake at the crest of the hill. They were safe. She smiled. And everything went black.

14

A BUMP SHOOK Adriane awake. She opened her eyes to darkness. The creaking of wheels and the hard floor bouncing beneath told her she was in some kind of wagon, rattling on a very bumpy road. She was all scrunched up, trapped in some kind of sack. She had no idea how long she'd been there, but the ache in her muscles felt like it had been a while.

"Hummmrr doo raahh . . ."

Someone was humming. It sounded awful . . . and awfully familiar.

"Hummmahuma Wahh wahh."

She tried to move, but the sharp pain in her shoulder made her stop. Carefully she reached around the back of her neck and felt a tender spot. She winced. Definitely a bruise, a big one. She flashed on a giant monster swatting her with a fist the size of a chair.

She moved her wrist in front of her face and focused on the wolf stone. Its soft light was weak, but enough to see she was in a large, black sack.

She heard sounds of sniffing and quickly covered her wrist, dousing the magic like a small flame.

"Ooo, you feel that?" the voice outside said. "Magic rock! Scorge is gonna get big reward. LaLaaaa!"

Scorge! That was why the humming sounded so familiar. It was that pesky orange . . . thing. And he thought *she* was a magic rock.

"Magic rock all right." He patted the bag as he happily hummed.

Adriane heard the sound of wheels on stone as the road smoothed. Suddenly, the wagon came to a creaky stop.

The sounds of shuffling and scuffling closed in about her. She braced herself. A door on the wagon opened and she was dragged out, still in the sack, and dumped onto a hard surface.

"Be careful of rock!" Scorge complained.

Heavy doors opened and she felt herself being dragged across sandy ground. The sound of the doors slamming shut echoed behind her. She had a bad feeling in the pit of her stomach as the ground tilted. She was going downhill.

Soon the ground leveled out. The echoing of footsteps and voices suggested she was in a large, enclosed space.

Something hit the floor next to her.

"Great Queenie, I have traveled long and far to bring you this great magic."

It was Scorge and he was groveling on the floor next to the sack. Adriane felt something cold press in around her, probing with the touch of magic. She stifled a gasp as ice stung at her wrist.

A voice, sharp as a razor, hissed, "You have brought what I seek?"

"Oh, yes! Great magic that has slept for thousand years," Scorge said between his constant thumping. He must be groveling up a storm.

"From another world, Your Mightiness," he continued. "Reward should only be as gigantic as Royal Highness thinks humble servant deserves."

"Show me this great magic," the cold voice ordered.

Adriane heard Scorge scamper to his feet. "M'lady . . . your magic rock!"

Adriane was jarred as the sack was lifted up, ripped open, and turned upside down.

She spilled out onto a cold, smooth floor.

Her muscles spasmed painfully as she tried to uncoil. Flashes sparked in her eyes in reaction to the sudden rush of light. She heard voices around the room snickering.

She could see Scorge's back. He was facing another figure. Long, flowing dark robes glided silently across the cold floor, moving closer.

"You!" the figure said.

"Me, me!" Scorge squealed and danced in delight—then saw that the tall figure was looking past him.

He turned and practically choked. "*You!*" Scorge sputtered, leaning down to press his dirty orange head into Adriane's face.

Adriane's thoughts were hazy. She could barely catch her breath.

"What you do with Scorge's rock—*graagah!*"

Scorge was swept away with a flick of the figure's wrist. He dropped to his knees, and pointed at Adriane. "That witch stole rock!" He began bowing and groveling again, shaking with fear.

Snickers turned to laughter.

"Silence!" The chamber fell deathly quiet at the icy command.

Adriane's mind cleared as her eyes adjusted to the light. At first, she thought she was in some kind of cathedral. The vast chamber rose to a high vaulted ceiling hidden in darkness. Then she realized those weren't stained glass windows; they were crystals imbedded in walls as if the entire place had been carved out of a mine.

She looked up at the robed figure in front of her. A hooded cloak shielded the features from view. Adriane knew who it was. The same terrifying figure that she,

Emily, and Kara had once seen at Ravenswood—at the portal. The Dark Sorceress.

"Where is my dragon?" the sorceress asked with a deadly calm.

"Um . . . dragon?" Scorge croaked.

She turned on him. "The dragon egg, you imbecile!"

"Er . . . dragon egg?"

"That *rock* is an egg! Or . . ." she turned to Adriane. " . . . it was an egg." She raised an arm in the air.

With a jolt, Adriane was forced to her feet. She tried to resist but couldn't control her own body. The sorceress looked her over carefully. She moved her arm, and like a puppet on a string, Adriane lifted her own arm, exposing the wolf stone.

"Interesting," the sorceress said.

"Very . . ." Scorge groveled. " . . . interesting!" He bowed some more. "Smaller rock, smaller reward . . ." he muttered.

The sorceress's sleeve slipped down her raised arm, revealing a hand with slender fingers tipped with long, sharp nails. She flexed, and the sharp claws slid back into her flesh.

Two figures moved behind Scorge. They were as tall as the sorceress, serpent like, with snake heads, and long, scaly bodies. They carried staffs that sparked with power.

"Take our guest and make sure he gets . . . what he deserves."

Scorge looked right and left, eyes widening. "Um . . .

Scorge change mind, don't need no reward*ghhh!*" A fist
had grabbed Scorge by his throat. And then the guards
were gone as quickly as they had appeared, Scorge with
them.

The sorceress pulled back her hood and advanced
toward Adriane. Strikingly beautiful, she had alabaster
skin like a porcelain doll, rich red lips, and long, white-
blond hair streaked with blazing bolts of silver lightning.
Then Adriane looked into her eyes. They were not
human, they were the eyes of an animal—no—some
creature—slit by vertical pupils, cold, dark, and pure evil.

"So it was you I felt at the portal," the sorceress said.

Adriane choked, sweat running down her face.

"Come, come, child, I know you can speak."

"Please . . . let . . . me go," Adriane managed to sputter.

"Oh, I'm sorry. Was I hurting you?"

As if the string holding her had snapped, Adriane fell
to the ground with a moan.

"Humans are such fragile things. Is that better?"

Adriane wiped spit from her mouth as she sat up. She
rubbed her arms and legs to get the circulation moving.
"Thank you."

"So polite." The sorceress circled Adriane, her silky
robes rustling lightly as she moved. "Do you know anything about magic? No. How could you? No one to train
you. Such a waste." She smiled and Adriane caught a
glimpse of vampire fangs. "Now . . ." The smile faded and
her eyes flashed like cold steel. "Where is my dragon?"

"I don't know," Adriane answered truthfully.

The eyes sparked dangerously. "Are you trying to make me upset? Is that what you want?" She flexed her hand, and the long, sharp claws slid out from her fingertips.

"I don't know where the dragon is." Adriane wobbled unsteadily to her feet, eyes carefully trained on the razor claws.

The sorceress continued to circle Adriane. "I have tracked the magic of the egg and I know it hatched. Then it just disappeared. Vanished . . . like mist." Her breath was cold as ice against Adriane's face. "Odd, don't you think?"

"I don't know."

The sorceress pointed a claw at her wolf stone. "Pity. Your stone is useless to me. It's been tuned to you. Just as the dragon has already imprinted on . . . whom?"

Adriane remained silent.

"But you are already bonded to a mistwolf, aren't you?"

Adriane said nothing.

"Aren't you?" The sorceress's eyes blazed into Adriane's.

"Yes," Adriane answered meekly. She couldn't turn away from those hypnotic eyes.

"Do you know that once a magical animal and a human are bonded, the bond is for life? One without the other is death to both. Did you know that?"

"Why—why are you telling me this?" Adriane stammered.

"So you know the truth. The animals are a burden and make you weak. Look at you now, you can barely stand up. All because you could not resist following the cry of the wolf."

Adriane stiffened.

"You think you are the first human magic user to try and help those pathetic Fairimentals by bonding with animals?" the sorceress said scornfully. "There have been many, and all have failed. The *truth* is the Fairimentals will use and manipulate you. And when you are used up, they will tell you how your spirit will be joined to the greater good of . . . Avalon."

She leaned in and hissed like a snake. "Avalon is not what you think it is."

She stepped back, her claws gleaming dangerously. "You are afraid to be here. You think this is all some perversion of the precious magic that binds you to these animals. Now amplify that fear a thousand fold and you have a small sense of what Avalon truly is. The only chance you have of actually entering Avalon is by working with me." Feral eyes blinded as a sly smile escaped her lips. "Give me what I need—what we need—to open the gates."

Adriane could feel the sorceress reach out her icy touch.

"Call the mistwolves. Bring them to me."

"No!"

"I wonder. Just how strong is your bond? Will your

mistwolf come for you? Or will she stand alone and watch you die?" She smiled evilly. "Let's see."

Instantly, Adriane was surrounded by serpent guards.

"Take her," the sorceress commanded, robes flying as she turned away.

Strong hands pulled Adriane toward a doorway. "I will never call the mistwolves!" she yelled.

"Then you will die," the sorceress said simply, then turned to her again. "Oh, how is your friend, Kara? I'm looking forward to meeting her again."

The sorceress's words echoed eerily as Adriane was dragged down a damp and musty tunnel. They passed open rooms, huge cavernous spaces cut into the earth, where dark figures worked on large crystals, sparks of fire flaring from the stones. The tunnel turned and twisted, going down into the earth. Adriane's heart pounded in her ears and her mind raced. These passageways all looked the same. She would never be able to find her way out of this place. The guards finally deposited Adriane in a wide room and she collapsed against a dank wall. Glints of light flashed off rock and crystal. She could feel energy flowing through the walls, pulsing like blood.

Adriane shivered, pulling her knees into her chest. She could hear moans in the darkness around her.

She got to her feet and held up her wolf stone, willing it to glow. Cutting a swatch of golden light in front of her, she saw rough crystal shapes jutting from the ceilings and cave floors. It was as if the entire place had formed right out of the earth itself. The light fell over a creature lying in the corner. Adriane moved closer and saw it was a pegasus, a winged pony, like the ones hidden at Ravenswood. This one was covered with ragged scars. Its wings were torn, green-glowing ooze on its back, sides, and legs. Black Fire.

Adriane edged closer and knelt before it, the light of her gem jittering.

The creature half opened its eyes. "Magic user . . ." It struggled to move.

"Shh, it's all right." Adriane tried to calm the creature, but she was shaking.

"Corintha . . ." it breathed.

"What?"

"Corintha . . . where is she?" It nodded weakly across the room.

Adriane got up and looked around, trying to steady the light as it swept across the room. It settled over the still body of another pegasus. There was no need to get any closer. She turned back. "I'm . . . sorry . . ."

The pegasus slumped. Tears ran from its eyes.

Something shuffled behind her. Other animals were slowly creeping out of the darkness. Adriane stifled a cry as her heart filled with anguish. There were dozens of creatures, some she recognized, like quiffles and jeeran, and some she didn't. The glint of golden cat eyes flashed as two big spotted cats emerged. They looked like Lyra—

before Emily had healed her. All the animals had the deathly glow of the Black Fire.

Adriane felt dizzy. Her stomach twisted into a knot. She felt as if she were suffocating.

"You are human."

She whirled around, and the light of her gemstone landed on a silver duck-like creature. It was a quiffle.

"Ye . . . yes."

"A human magic user!" another of the animals exclaimed.

Adriane heard the whispers from one to another as the word spread. A human was here among them. And she carried magic!

More animals crowded into the room.

Adriane didn't know what to do.

She felt in her pocket for the last of the coconuts. She took it out. These creatures were starving—how was this going to help?

Trying to control her shaking, she carefully broke the coconut into small pieces and began handing them out.

"I'm sorry, it's all I have," she said miserably. She was desperately fighting to keep herself from breaking down and losing it completely.

"Packmate . . ." a soft voice said in her mind.

Adriane jumped. The light of her gem began to pulse. She strained to hear the voice.

"You are not alone."

It was a mistwolf. Adriane knew it instinctively.

And the wolf was somewhere close, calling from the shadows of the prison.

She held up her gem and scanned the dark corners.

"Is there a mistwolf here?" she asked the animals, her voice trembling.

"Yes," one of the quiffles said. "She is dying."

"Take me to her. Please!" Adriane pleaded.

While the rest of the animals shared the small coconut, Adriane followed the quiffle under a low archway into another chamber. In the center was a clear box. As Adriane got closer, she saw it was a cage made completely of glass. And inside, curled on the floor, lay a silver mistwolf.

Adriane ran to the cage and placed her hands on the glass. Her stone flared wildly.

The wolf was ragged and weak, her rib cage sharply outlined through her skin. Patches of her once lustrous fur were gone, revealing burnt flesh crisscrossed with ugly green lines. As the light of Adriane's gem flashed over her, the wolf weakly raised her head, eyes half opened.

"It is good to see you."

Adriane's heart felt like it was being ripped apart. Anger welled, surging inside with the force of a hurricane. Filled with rage, she pounded her fist, spilling golden fire onto the glass.

The glass cracked, but held.

She turned to see the other animals watching her.

The animals huddled together and moved closer. She felt the weakness within them, overcome by the dark force of Black Fire. It ran through them, infecting their magic.

Still, she drew whatever strength they could offer.

Adriane screamed as a wave of green light swept from the animals and into her jewel. She threw the power at the glass. It shattered.

Crossing the scattered shards, she knelt and carefully lifted the wolf's head into her lap, gently stroking the mottled fur.

Everything she had experienced—the loss of the griffin, the dead wilderbeasts on the hill, the rivers of poison tearing across the land, the monstrous creatures, and now, these animals, alone and lost, dying—came pouring out at once.

Adriane's tears fell like rain as she hugged the mistwolf.

She thought about Storm, strong, vibrant, and full of life. She knew she couldn't call her. She could never bear to have Storm end up here. And suddenly Adriane realized why she had come all this way. Why she had risked everything to find her friend. All she wanted, needed, was the chance to say I love you . . . and to say good-bye.

Adriane cried until there were no more tears left.

"Your mistwolf loves you very much," the gentle voice said in her head.

Adriane gazed into her soft silvery blue eyes.

Although the wolf's body was wracked with poison, her eyes were clear and full of compassion.

"I miss her so much," Adriane sniffled.

"Shh, little one. No matter how far, she is always in your heart, as you are in hers."

Adriane curled into the mistwolf's side, snuggling close. She saw her wolf stone sparking from gold to green and knew that the poison was starting to spread through her own body as well. She refused to remove it. If this was the end, this was how she wanted to go.

"My name is Adriane," she said to the wolf.

"I am Silver Eyes."

Suddenly the air began to sparkle. Then she heard that unmistakable sound.

Pop! Pop! Pop! Pop! Pop!

15

FIVE BRIGHTLY COLORED dragonflies popped into the cave, red, orange, blue, yellow, and purple. They took one look at Adriane and the other animals, gave a chorus of shrieks, and immediately disappeared.

"Wait!" Adriane called out after them. "Come back . . . ohhh."

She couldn't blame them. She was among dozens of sick animals, a dying mistwolf by her side, and she could feel the Black Fire moving at a deadly pace through her body.

"Silver Eyes," she said to the mistwolf, "we thought you were dead."

She heard a soft bark, which Adriane recognized as a wolf laugh. *"Not yet."*

"Zachariah thinks so, too."

"Zachariah?" The wolf's eyes opened wide. *"Little Wolf?"*

"Little Wolf?" Adriane asked. "A human boy, he was raised—"

The wolf struggled to sit up. *"Is he all right?"*

"Yes, the last time I saw him."

"You saw my human son?" Her voice was full of wonder.

"Yes."

The wolf lay her head back down in Adriane's arms. *"Little Wolf is all right . . ."* She repeated over and over.

"He thinks it was his fault," Adriane told her.

"It was not his fault."

"Moonshadow thinks so."

"Moonshadow is the most stubborn creature in Aldenmor!"

Adriane smiled.

"He could never accept the boy as his pack brother."

"Moonshadow is taking the pack somewhere safe," Adriane said. "My friend, Stormbringer, is with them. She thought she was the last mistwolf. Then we found the others."

"A wolf is bound to protect the pack," Silver Eyes said. *"But that does not mean she has abandoned you."*

"Then why did she leave?"

"Sometimes you have to leave to find your way home."

Pop! Pop! Pop! Pop! Pop!

The dragonflies were back, this time huddled together in a tight ball, shaking and squeaking.

Adriane slowly got to her feet and extended her arms. "It's all right. Don't be afraid."

Fiona broke away and landed, trembling, on Adriane's arm. "Ooo, Deedee!" Fiona's little red eyes swirled with distress.

"It's okay, Fiona. Did you bring me another message?"

She leaped into the air and chirped at the others. There was some confusing dragonfly chitter, and a few angry squeaks. Then they linked front wing claws together and started to spin in a colorful circle.

"Too Kaaraa!" Goldie squeaked.

Suddenly the area inside their circle began to sparkle.

The dragonflies had made a window about the size of a dinner plate—they had opened a small portal! Adriane peeked in and saw a hairy nose and a few whiskers.

She stepped back, confused.

Then she heard a familiar voice.

"I can't tell if this is working or not! Dooh! Those pesky things!" It was Ozzie!

"Ozzie!" she called out.

"Huh?" The hairy face pulled back and she could see Ozzie's whole ferret head. His little brown eyes opened wide in astonishment.

"Adriane!" He started hopping up and down, yelling over his shoulder. "I've got her! Hurry!"

Adriane couldn't believe it. She was looking through a window into the library at Ravenswood Manor. She heard the sounds of shuffling and running.

"Adriane!" It was Emily!

"Emily!" Adriane cried out, fresh tears streaming down her face. "I'm here!"

Ozzie's snout was pushed aside as Emily's face filled the little window.

Adriane was filled with joy. "It's my friends," she called out to the other animals.

Emily's face lit up, then changed to shock. "Adriane, what happened to you?"

Suddenly Kara's blond head pressed in tight against Emily's auburn curls. "You look terrible!"

"I missed you, too." Adriane didn't know whether to laugh or cry, so she did both.

The dragonflies' circle began weaving about as they argued among themselves. The window ghosted and flickered like a bad television signal.

"Oh, no," Adriane cried.

"Hey! Keep spinning!" Kara yelled at the dragonflies.

"OOoooOO!" Instantly the dragonflies stopped arguing and returned to spinning in a synchronized circle. The picture cleared.

Emily and Kara were looking at Adriane. Ozzie was jumping up and down on the desk, trying to get a look as Lyra paced behind them. Adriane could not remember ever feeling so happy. "How is Gran?" she asked.

"Fine," Kara said. "We told her you were staying at the Pet Palace helping Dr. Fletcher."

"Adriane, where are you?" Emily's face was full of concern. "What's happened to you?"

Adriane could only imagine what she must look like. She was filthy, her hair straggly and matted, the left side of her neck, purpled with welts. She could feel the Black Fire slowly creeping through her.

"Okay now, don't freak out . . ."

Her friends all held their breath.

"I'm in the sorceress's dungeon."

"What?" Kara and Emily looked at each other. Lyra growled behind them. Ozzie fell off the desk with a loud crash.

"There are a lot of sick animals here, and there's a mistwolf. She's hurt so bad . . ."

"What about you?" Emily asked, cutting her off.

Adriane lowered her head. "The poison is in me too."

"GAHaaaah!" She heard Ozzie scream.

"What do we do?" Kara yelled, grabbing Emily.

Lyra yowled and Ozzie began leaping like a frog. The dragonflies squealed—and their circle began to flutter apart.

"Stop it!" Emily's voice cut through the commotion. "Chill! Everyone! Let me think!"

She turned to Kara. "Keep those dragonflies spinning!"

Kara yelled into the window, "Listen up!"

"Ooo!"

"Keep this window open no matter what! Got it?"

"Ookies, Kaaraa," Goldie squeaked.

"Adriane, let me see your wolf stone," Emily said.

Adriane held up her stone and Emily gasped. The once-bright gold and amber tiger's eye now glowed with a sickly green hue.

"Kara, Lyra, over here! Now!" Emily raised her rainbow jewel. Lyra and Kara were at her side in a flash.

"You, too, Ozzie."

The ferret leaped onto the big cat's head.

"Stand still, Adriane!"

Emily held up her jewel and concentrated. It flashed with cool blue light. "Kara, give me your hand," she said.

Emily and Kara joined hands as Lyra and Ozzie crowded in even closer.

"Concentrate on healing . . . feel Adriane's heartbeat and lock it on your own. Steady, strong, until our hearts beat as one."

The dragonflies squeaked softly, but kept spinning their magic window in front of Adriane.

"Now!"

Blue fire shot from Emily's jewel right through the window and slammed into Adriane's wolf stone. Adriane was thrown back. The dragonflies shrieked and broke their circle. The picture in the window sputtered, blinking in and out.

"Keep spinning!" Kara commanded.

Goldie sparked a golden flame and yelled at the others. They clasped wing claws again and spun. The window cleared.

Adriane's stone pulsed erratically, blinking from green to gold and back to green.

"Again!" Emily yelled.

Everyone concentrated and the magic leaped from the rainbow jewel, through the window, blazing into the wolf stone. Waves of blue light ran up and down Adriane's arms and began to spread, bathing her in pure healing magic.

Emily jerked back her arm and the blue light of the jewel faded.

Adriane stood, her arm raised, the wolf stone flashing golden light. "It's gone! You did it!"

A cheer went up from the animals in the dark cave.

Squealing with joy, the dragonflies started dancing and swooping, breaking their circle—causing the window to flicker and fall apart.

"Hey!" Kara yelled. "Not you! Keep spinning!"

"Ooop!" The dragonflies jumped back together and spun.

"Okay, Kara, can you move the dragonflies around the room so I can see the animals?" Emily asked.

"You heard her—start moving. Slowly!" Kara called out.

With a few squeaks, the dragonflies slowly spun their window over the animals.

Adriane quickly rounded up the wounded creatures in the dungeon, separating them according to how serious their injuries were. When the dragonflies flew over Silver Eyes, Emily studied the mistwolf closely.

Emily raised her rainbow jewel in the air. "Okay. She's

first. Just like before. I need everyone's help. Stay close and focused."

"Right!" Kara, Ozzie, and Lyra stood ready.

"Adriane, are you ready?" Emily asked.

"Let's do it!" Adriane said, her wolf stone raised

"A walk in the park," Emily raised her jewel. "Here we go . . . Now!"

Blue-white magic exploded out of Emily's rainbow jewel and shot straight through the window, wrapping the wolf in a cocoon of light.

Golden fire flew from Adriane's stone and enveloped the blue. With all her might, she willed the wolf to heal. Blue and gold lights flared brighter and brighter until they were a blinding white glow.

"Enough!" Emily shouted.

They lowered their gems and the light slowly faded from the wolf.

Adriane helped Silver Eyes to her feet. The wolf was still weak and thin, her fur still mottled, but there was no trace of the Black Fire anywhere on her body! Adriane's heart soared as she knelt to hug the wolf. "You're going to be all right."

Another cheer went up from the animals as Adriane turned to them, smiling. Tears of joy ran down her cheeks. "We have to hurry before the sorceress feels this magic," she said.

"I will use my magic to shield us," Silver Eyes said, as she slowly evaporated into mist.

One by one, Emily, Adriane, and Kara healed each animal through the dragonflies' spinning window. The process went faster and faster as the healthy animals added their pure magic to the healing. Others too weak to walk were carried in. Soon, every animal in the dungeon was healed.

Adriane's eyes shone as she looked at her friends through the dragonflies' window. "We did it!" she cried.

"Can you get everyone out of there?" Emily asked.

"It's an underground maze," a doglike creature said. "No one's ever gotten out of here."

The animals fell silent.

"*I have.*" Lyra was looking into the window.

"*Lyra?*" a voice called from the crowd of animals.

"*Rynda?*" Lyra began scanning the animals.

A large, spotted cat stepped forward.

"*My sister!*" Lyra yowled. "*Where is Olinde?*"

Another cat pushed through the group. "*I'm here.*"

"*I thought you were lost,*" Lyra said.

"*And now we are found,*" the cats mewed.

"Can you help us get out?" a quiffle asked Lyra.

"*I escaped the dungeons. Listen to my thoughts, Rynda.*"

Rynda closed her cat eyes.

"*Look into my mind. Can you see the path I took?*"

"*Yes, sister,*" the cat said.

She turned to the animals. "*This way,*" Rynda directed, and led them out of the chamber and into the dark tunnels.

Adriane saw her friends in the window back at Ravenswood.

Kara, Emily, Lyra, and Ozzie all stared back.

"Keep the faith," she said to them. "I will come home!"

With a quick series of *pops,* the dragonflies vanished.

"We love you, Adriane!" her friends called out as the window faded. And they were gone.

"I love you, too," Adriane said and followed the animals.

With Rynda in the lead, the entire group moved up through the tunnels. Adriane ran alongside, senses on high alert. As they passed a small cave, she heard a moan.

She ducked into the opening, golden gem held high.

Scorge lay chained to a wall. He looked even more wretched and pathetic than usual. "Scorge is so doomed. Oh, me, me," he moaned.

Despite what he had done to her, Adriane couldn't leave him here. She flung out a stream of magic and broke open the old rusty chains with one swipe. Scorge's eyes opened wide and he fell to his knees, groveling.

"Oh, thank you, thank you. You are good witch. Scorge is humble servant . . ."

"You're on your own now. Good luck." She turned and ran after the others.

Tunnel after tunnel, twist after turn, the group followed Rynda upward, toward the surface. Occasionally they had to sneak by large caverns occupied with workers, but nothing stopped them. No one expected the prisoners to ever attempt an escape.

Finally the floor leveled out and the tunnel ended at a large set of doors.

Adriane held her hand up to silence everyone. Then, slowly, she pushed open the doors. Outside was an open, stone-paved yard, and beyond it, the barren gray landscape of the Shadowlands. Night had fallen, and she could see the twin moons rising into the starry sky.

Four serpent guards marched back and forth across the yard.

Adriane walked out right between them. "Say, is this where the bus stops for Stonehill?"

The guards turned on her at once, staffs raised. Green fire licked from the tips, and they charged.

Suddenly they skidded to a stop, shock on their serpentine faces. Behind Adriane thirty animals came charging out the door. Adriane whipped out golden fire and yanked the staffs into the air as the animals raced forward, barreling over the surprised guards.

Adriane led the triumphant group across the yard and onto a stretch of flat, sandy ground. Behind them, several small volcanoes were rising from the desert. There were doors at the bases of each. She wondered briefly if she had come out the same place she'd gone in.

All around them lay the forbidding Shadowlands. Adriane held her wolf stone out in front of her. Which way should she go? They needed to get as far away as fast as they could. It would not be long before the sorceress learned of their escape.

"Follow my voice!"

Adriane's heart soared. "Storm!"

"I am with you." The voice of the mistwolf rang clear and true in her mind.

Adriane saw a line of dunes ahead, dark against the night sky.

"This way!" she yelled, herding the group toward the distant dunes.

Under the bright light of two moons, the animals fled across the parched sands. Adriane was out front, her wolf stone flashing in the night, a beacon to lead them.

"Storm!" she called.

Suddenly her gemstone flashed, and Adriane's mind whirled. Once again she was being pulled into the mind of the wolf. She breathed in fresh night air, felt sand beneath her padded feet, but saw no pack. Instead, only the image of a single figure. Slowly it came into focus. It was human. It was . . . *her!* Adriane was looking through Storm's eyes and seeing *herself.*

She blinked and saw a lone wolf standing strong, silhouetted by the light of the rising moons.

"Stormbringer!" Adriane cried. She ran to her friend and hugged her hard, as if she'd never let go.

The mistwolf licked her face. *"You found me."*

The light of the moons suddenly went dark, then brightened. A large shadow flew across the sky. Adriane felt her stone pulse with danger.

The animals began cowering and whispering. They felt it, too. Something was coming . . .

With a sound like thunder, the ground shook.

Something was here.

Behind the animals, a shape stood, unfurling immense bat wings, each with pointed razor tips. The demon's huge muscles rippled along a body covered in thick leather armor. Its eyes blazed red. Green venom dripped from its set of long razor teeth as it smiled.

A vision out of her worst nightmare stepped forward and Adriane's heart sank.

The manticore roared and leaped straight for them.

16

THE ANIMALS SCREAMED and scattered as the manticore landed with a ground-shaking *crunch* not ten feet in front of them and straightened to its full height. Armored in dark leather, its lower body looked like a mutated lion; the upper part resembled some bizarre ape-beast, with arms muscled like steel cords. A thick tail, tipped with iron spikes, swayed dangerously behind it.

"We meet again." The monster's guttural voice grated like shards of metal. "What magic do you have for me this time?" it challenged.

Adriane realized it was toying with them, reminding her that it had attacked once before, at Ravenswood, and had stolen the fairy map. It had taken the magic of the three girls working together to send the monster back through the portal.

Now she faced it alone.

No! She was not alone. Storm stood by her side, the bond between them strong and true. And her friends, Emily, Kara, Ozzie, and Lyra—they were with her, always.

"Let us go!" she yelled.

The demon snarled. "I was told to bring you back alive. But accidents happen."

"Stay away from us!"

The manticore stepped forward.

Adriane raised her wolf stone high, her other hand gripping the thick fur of Storm's ruff. The silver wolf snarled, teeth bared. Golden fire flared from Adriane's fist, spiraling down her arm, and covering her entire body. She and Storm stood bright as flames in the desert darkness and sent a beam of white-gold magic flying into the manticore.

The power slammed into the creature hard, forcing it back. The manticore roared. Together, Adriane and Storm whipped the magic around the manticore, wrapping the monster in fire.

The beast stood in the magical inferno—and smiled. Then it opened its blood-red mouth and took a long, deep breath. A ribbon of gold snaked its way into the manticore's mouth. It was inhaling the magic!

Adriane was suddenly jerked forward.

"Storm!"

The mistwolf leaped in front of Adriane and snapped at the manticore, looking for an opening to attack.

The manticore opened its mouth wider and began swallowing the magic. Adriane was being pulled in. She tried to resist but it was too strong.

Golden light flew wildly into the creature's nose, its mouth, and its ears. Then, with its chest fully expanded, the manticore heaved, spewing sickly green light back at Adriane.

From the corner of her eye, she saw all the animals closing in, trying to give her what magic they had.

"No!" she called to them. "Stay away!"

Like a bullet, Storm streaked for the manticore's back, hitting it from behind. Teeth imbedded in leather and flesh, the wolf violently shook its head. The monster roared and twisted around, trying to dislodge its attacker.

It was enough of a distraction. Adriane pushed back, trying to keep the green fire from flowing into her gem. The beam of light warped, angling sharply into the air. She twisted her wrist, trying to cut off the flow. With all her strength, Adriane smacked the beam down hard, cutting a smoking rift into the ground. Sand and rocks went flying as the magic burst apart, shooting sparks of lightning into the air. Her stone free from the creature's grip, Adriane tumbled backward.

With a flap of its dark wings, the manticore suddenly rose into the air, throwing Storm to the ground. With a booming thud, the creature landed behind the frightened animals.

The animals went running in chaos and confusion over to Adriane and Storm.

The manticore slowly looked over the huddled, shaking group.

"Healthy animals for the mistress to begin her work again. You did well." Its eyes focused on Adriane. "She cannot use your stone. But I can. You will have no use for it back in the dungeons."

The manticore closed its wings to reveal a regiment of armored serpent guards, one hundred strong, marching across the sands. The animals gasped and cried as the serpents fanned out into a line as they approached, and then came to a halt. The thudding sound of a hundred staffs pounding the ground echoed across the terrified group. Each serpent held its staff in front of them, pointed at the sky. Green sparks leaped into the night from the tips.

"Your magic is strong, but you cannot win," the manticore said.

The animals pressed tightly around Adriane and Storm, trembling, eyes darting about nervously.

Adriane leaned against Storm, wrapping both arms around the mistwolf. She was drained. She felt as if everything was slipping away, out of reach—except for one thing. The thing that mattered most.

"Storm," she said softly, her face buried in the wolf's neck. "You came for me. You risked everything for me."

"You did the same for me."

"Moonshadow was right. I have only brought you danger. Go. Please!" she begged. "Save yourself."

The wolf nuzzled Adriane's cheek. *"I would not be able to go on without you."*

"Really?"

"Yes."

"I love you, Storm."

"And I love you, Adriane."

An eerie howl split the night, echoing across the desert.

Adriane's eyes widened.

Another howl, then another swept over them like a ghostly chorus of ancient spirits.

Suddenly Storm raised her head to the moons and howled in response. Standing up, Adriane threw back her head and howled alongside her friend.

One by one, the animals added their voices, sending the wolfsong over the desert and back into the night.

The booming roar of thunder rolled over them, washing out the cries.

A huge thundercloud, black and gray, was moving down the dunes toward them. The cloud spilled across the sand and began to form into individual shapes—wolves. The entire pack racing straight for them.

And behind them, Adriane saw something else.

It was Zach, his Elven sword drawn to protect the big red baby dragon that lumbered beside him. The dragon craned his neck, straining to push forward, looking for something.

"They come!" The manticore roared to his serpent troops. "Tonight we will finish this. Ready!"

As one, the serpents raised their staffs high and pointed at the oncoming wolves. Green fire sparked from one tip to the next, racing across the line of weapons and joining into a single web of roiling fire.

Adriane looked in horror from the wolves back to the serpents as the truth suddenly hit her.

It was a trap! She had brought the mistwolves and the dragon to the sorceress. She was responsible.

No wonder it had been so easy to escape the dungeons. The sorceress needed *live* bait.

"Remember, we want them undamaged!" the manticore's voice boomed.

"No! Go back!" Adriane screamed at the charging wolves. She whirled to Storm. "Tell them!"

But it was too late. The serpent army stepped forward . . . and fired.

Green lightning lit the night skies as the fiery net flew forward from the line of staffs. As the wolves drew nearer, the net spread wide, ready to engulf the onrushing pack.

The manticore's eyes blazed with triumph. "Yes!"

The net fell to the sandy ground in a haze of sparks.

The manticore's eyes flew open in rage as the serpents began looking around frantically. Thirty animals and a hundred mistwolves had just suddenly vanished from sight.

From under the misty veil, Adriane knew exactly what had happened. At the last moment, the entire pack had dissolved into mist. The magic of the mistwolves had settled over the animals, making them invisible to anyone outside.

"Maamaa!"

The Drake bounded into Adriane's arms, covering her face in warm, wet dragon licks.

"Drake!" she cried happily. "I'm so glad you're okay."

"Find them!" the manticore screamed. Through the cloud, Adriane could see the manticore stomping around, enraged. It was searching for them, sweeping the sand into clouds with its huge wings.

"Hurry!" The voices of the wolves filled the veil. *"We must move quickly."*

Under the magic mist of the wolves, the animals huddled close behind Adriane, Storm, and the Drake, and began to move away.

Green flashes erupted around them as the serpents fired random blasts at the ground.

Adriane held up her stone and focused on the light at its center. Yellow-gold flashed. Concentrating hard, she sent a ghost image of her gemstone to a spot on the far side of the guards.

"Over there!" one yelled, as a gold light sparked in the

distance. They started running toward the false magic signal—away from their prey.

The manticore sniffed at the air and turned its head. Slit demon eyes looked directly at the place where Adriane and the others were hidden. Adriane held her breath. With a low growl, the manticore started for them—but stopped.

Adriane saw Zach standing in front of the monster, sword out and ready.

"We can't leave without Zach!" she cried.

The manticore snarled and grabbed for the boy. Silver steel stung the beast's arm and it roared in pain, lashing out. Zach leaped out of the way. Spinning around, he sliced into the manticore's leg, sword flashing. The creature swung its body, plowing giant arms at the boy's head. Zach ducked, but he was slammed to the ground by the beast's iron-spiked tail. The boy shook his head, pushed himself up, and tried to get to his feet.

The monster raised a giant foot and roared. "I will kill you as easily as I killed your parents, boy!"

"Then you will have to kill me as well."

A large shape materialized in the air as it flew at the monster, knocking it back and taking it down. It was a wolf, huge and black. The manticore fell with a booming crash as it tried to throw the wolf off. But the wolf was too stubborn and held on, raking its claws down the creature's chest, locking teeth into its neck.

Adriane saw a sparkling orb dangling from the black wolf's neck. It was Moonshadow.

The manticore writhed and struggled, pulling at the wolf with massive hands. It ripped the wolf free and threw him to the ground. The monster twisted to its knees and raised a giant fist—but Zach was much faster. He lunged forward, plunging the sword deep into the manticore's side.

The monster screamed as green blood burst from the wound.

Wolf and boy stood side by side, watching the monster stagger to its feet, open its wings, and lift into the sky, trying to stem its lifeblood from spilling out into the sands.

Zach stepped forward, eager to finish the monster, but Moonshadow stopped him.

"Another time, brother," the wolf said. *"We must protect the others."*

Zach looked at his wolf brother, sheathed his sword, and gave a short nod. Together they ran toward Adriane and the animals and entered the cloud of mist.

"Move. Now!" Moonshadow commanded.

Once again, the group started walking into the desert.

Zach ran to Adriane's side, his face full of concern. "Adriane, are you all right?"

"Yes." She smiled. "You rescued me again."

He smiled back, and his face blushed bright red. Then his eyes opened wide as he looked past her.

A wolf stepped forward from the group of animals. Silver Eyes.

Zach and Moonshadow started toward her at the same time, then the pack leader nodded his head, and the boy ran to embrace his wolf mother.

"I thought I'd never see you again," he cried into her fur.

"And I, too, Little Wolf, my son."

They raised their heads and looked to Moonshadow. The great black wolf stepped close and touched his nose to Silver Eyes' cheek.

"My heart soars with happiness, my wolf mother."

"As does mine, Moonshadow, my son."

Adriane looked on happily, Storm on one side of her, the Drake on the other.

Moonshadow and Zach, Silver Eyes between them, stepped forward to lead the group. Everyone followed, moving quickly between the dunes.

"How do we find our way?" Adriane asked.

"The gift from the Fairimentals will show us," Moonshadow told her.

Adriane saw the sparkling lights of the orb that hung from the pack leader's neck. He led the entire group into a shallow ravine beyond the far side of the dunes. The mist-covered group entered the hidden portal and vanished in a blinding white light.

17

"**H**OLD STILL!" ADRIANE said, tying a vine under the wolf's chin. She adjusted the big, bright blue leaf in place atop Storm's head.

"Why do I have to wear this silly thing?" the wolf complained.

"Because it's a party. We all wear them." She grinned at the thought of the lovely lavender leaf draped over her head at a rakish angle. Even Kara would be impressed at this Fairy Glen fashion statement.

Adriane and Storm sat together by the shores of the sparkling blue lake. It was a beautiful morning and Adriane felt clean and refreshed, having spent practically two hours scrubbing every inch of her body in the cool, clean waters.

"Storm . . ."

"*Yes.*"

"I was hurt when you left . . ." Glints of sunlight played across the crystal waters. "But I understand why you had to come here." She gazed at her friend. "What the mistwolves can do here, helping the Fairimentals and everyone in Aldenmor, is so much more important than . . . well, what I'm trying to say is . . ." She cast her eyes down and tried to be strong. "If you want to stay here, I want you to, also."

Storm nudged Adriane's cheek with her nose and licked the girl's face. "*Warrior,*" the wolf said. "*Thank you. Let us see what the pack decides.*"

"Okay." Adriane smiled. Grabbing an armful of leaves, she got to her feet. "Come on."

The sun shone brightly through the trees as they walked down a path to an open meadow.

Rainbow sparkles spiraled in the air. Adriane watched the Drake open his beautiful red wings. They shimmered in colors. With a great flap, the dragon succeeded in lifting himself off the ground for a few seconds, then crashed, playfully rolling in the heather. A moment later, he popped up again like a giant red kitten, trying to grab a gleefully singing breeze that hovered just out of his reach. The Air Fairimental giggled as she danced around the dragon.

"Yeah! Stretch your wings. That's it." Zach circled, watching the Drake intently. "That's really good."

The dragon hopped up and down excitedly and promptly rolled over on his back. Zach plopped down and rubbed his round belly. The dragon crooned happily, his big legs running in the air.

Adriane had her hand over her mouth, trying to hold back her laughter.

Zach looked up at her. "What? He likes his tummy rubbed."

Adriane smiled. "You two were meant for each other, you know that?"

Zach smiled back. "He belches louder than I do."

Adriane sighed as she and Storm walked over. "Here, put this on." She carefully tied a big, floppy yellow leaf onto Zach's head.

"Do I have to?"

"Yes!" She wagged a finger at him. "Don't make me mad, now!"

The Drake gazed hopefully at her with his big, puppy-dog eyes.

"One for you, too." She tied a purple leaf between his horns.

A wet forked tongue licked her forehead.

She stepped back and admired the three of them, Storm, Zach, and Drake. "Perfect. C'mon, let's go."

As they headed down the path, Adriane moved up behind Zach and covered his eyes.

"Hey!"

"Shhh, it's a *surprise* party." She giggled.

Only when they entered Okawa's meadow did she take her hands away.

Under the giant branches of the huge tree, all the animals had gathered. Cats, quiffles, pegasi, even two small wilderbeasts. They cheered as Zach stood, his mouth open in surprise. Ambia hovered next to Gwigg beside a wooden platform piled high with fruits, coconuts, and a tall layer cake that sparkled with tiny, sugary lights.

A pegasus pony with blue-and-white wings stepped forward. "It was the most daring rescue ever in the history of Aldenmor!" it exclaimed.

"This day will be remembered always," a hamster-sized dog said.

"We will compose many songs for you, warrior," a rubbery-beaked quiffle said to Adriane.

Adriane smiled. "Well, in the meantime, do you remember the one I taught you?"

"Sort of."

"Okay, then, all together now . . ." She raised her arms to conduct the animal chorus. They all sang out as best they could, a cacophony of animal voices—hoots and neighs, growls and chirps, hollers and hums.

"Happy birth today you, happy you to birth, too, happy day haay, hey you hoot, happy birthday to you, too!"

The animals stopped and waited expectantly. Zach looked happily bemused.

Adriane clapped, laughing. "Wonderful!"

Cheers filled the meadow.

Zach bowed graciously. "Thank you, all."

Adriane stood in front of him and held out a bright package wrapped in yellow and pink leaves.

"What's that?" he asked.

"It's your birthday present."

"Say, how do you know it's really my birthday?"

"Because I said so. Here, open it."

Zach took the small package and looked at it. He held it to his ear and shook it.

Adriane rolled her eyes.

He smiled and unwrapped the carefully folded leaves. His eyes widened as he took out a red stone. It was round and rough-edged, but the tiny, faceted crystals in the center flowed with red fire. "It's . . . it's . . ."

"I found it in the Drake's egg. The Fairimentals confirmed it. It's a dragon stone."

"I can't take this!" he whispered in wonder and sudden fear.

"Yes you can, Zach." She put her hands on his and closed them over the dragon stone. It pulsed with red light. At her wrist, the wolf stone sparkled in response. "Make it yours," she smiled.

Zach broke out in a wide grin. He held the stone up high so everyone could see. "It's a dragon stone!"

Everyone cheered.

"Tummy rubb!"

"Huh?" Zach stared at Drake in amazement. The

dragon was lying on his back, gazing at Zach expectantly. "What did you say?"

"Tickle, Zaaakk!"

"Hey, I can hear him!" He grinned at Adriane. "This is the best present ever!"

She looked past him. "Zach . . ."

He turned around and saw Moonshadow and Silver Eyes standing with Ambia and Gwigg. He walked over to join them.

"You have a leaf on your head," Moonshadow observed.

Zach blushed. "It's my birthday."

The black wolf cocked his head curiously.

"Happy birthday, son," Silver Eyes said.

Adriane and Storm joined them.

Moonshadow lightly pawed the ground and then spoke. *"It has been decided."* The black wolf's keen eyes moved from the Fairimentals to the animals.

Everyone waited.

"With the safe return of our pack mother to guide us, we will put aside our differences. The mistwolves will stay and work with the Fairimentals."

The animals gave a resounding cheer.

"What about Storm?" Adriane asked, her heart suddenly beating faster.

"The choice is hers," Moonshadow's gaze settled on Storm.

Storm stepped forward and addressed the wolves. *"Since I was a pup I have dreamed of running with the pack.*

But the bond I made with my human packmate makes me who I am. My heart beats with hers." The wolf stepped to Adriane's side. *"I belong with her."*

Joy filled Adriane's heart.

"You are always welcome here, packmate," Silver Eyes said to Storm, and then looked at Adriane. *"As are you . . . wolf sister."*

Silver Eyes turned to Moonshadow. The black wolf pawed the ground then lifted his head to Adriane. *"You honor us, warrior."*

Adriane smiled and bowed to the pack leader. "The honor is mine."

"There is much to be done." Ambia hovered by Adriane's side. "You must continue your work with your friends. The magic web is full of mysteries and the search for Avalon must continue."

"We will continue our work to protect Aldenmor," Gwigg said. "Together."

Moonshadow nodded to Zach. *"My brother's fight is my fight."*

"Good, then you'll need this." Zach quickly pulled a giant pink leaf hat over Moonshadow's head.

The black wolf snarled, shaking his head. *"I am not wearing that!"*

"Oh, yes you are!"

The boy tussled with the wolf, trying to pull the hat onto his head.

"Oh, no, I am not!"

Moonshadow pulled the boy down and they rolled around in the grass, struggling with the leaf.

Silver Eyes looked at Adriane with a twinkle in her eyes. *"Boys, what can you do?"*

"Adriane," Ambia said, her fresh voice cool and breezy. "You have proved yourself far beyond what we could have hoped for."

"Close your eyes and picture what you want most," Gwigg rumbled.

Adriane closed her eyes.

A gust of wind blew across the meadow, filling it with soft, twinkly lights. The lights swirled into a glowing circle that expanded before them. Everyone looked in wonder as a picture formed inside. It was a grassy field. Two girls, a large cat, and a small furry creature stood there waiting.

"Emily, Kara, Ozzie, Lyra!" Adriane called out, waving.

"Adriane!" Emily yelled, looking back through the portal.

"Gahhh! It's the Fairy Glen!" Ozzie started hopping about excitedly.

Zach peered into the portal curiously.

"Who's that?" Kara asked, tilting her blond head forward to get a better look.

"Are you all right?" Emily asked.

"Who is that?" Kara persisted.

"This is my friend, Zach," Adriane said.

"Hello."

"Helllooo," Kara called out. "Nice souvenir, girl!"

Adriane turned to Zach. "You could come with me . . ." she said.

"No, I belong here. This is my home." He hugged her. "Thank you, Adriane."

"Hey, remember me?" Ozzie was jumping up and down.

"Ozymandius," Ambia called to him. "The things you do for us do not go unnoticed."

"Well, that's nice, but I itch!"

Ambia fluttered over Adriane. "Adriane, what is it you most desire?"

With one hand on Storm, she turned to her friends at Ravenswood. "I just want to go home."

Together, Adriane and Storm stepped through the portal and went over the rainbow.

Bestiary &
Creature Guide

DRAGON

AFFILIATION: NEUTRAL

An ancient, winged reptilian race known and feared for their size, physical prowess, and powerful magic. Fast and sleek, there are few creatures that can keep up with a dragon in flight. Dragons usually only associate with other dragons, but the rare mage that bonds with one finds exceptional empathic understanding and fierce loyalty.

Dragons are thought to be extinct on Aldenmor, but it is rumored they have hidden themselves in Dragon Home, located in an isolated place on the web.

GRIFFIN

*H*alf-lion, half-eagle, griffins are ferocious avian carnivores. Though not as fast or sleek as other flyers, a griffin's muscled lion's body allows exceptional endurance and stamina for long distances.

Keen eagle eyesight and sense of smell make griffins excellent trackers.

Griffins are brave and very loyal to those mages lucky enough to bond with one.

IMPS

*D*iminutive members of the Demon class, imps
are formed by twisted, electrical magical currents
that hold their oily jet black forms together. If
injured, they can re-form themselves or merge
together into larger forms. Imps have no individual
thought, they act as a unit and follow one group
prerogative.

GARGOYLE

*W*inged medium size member of the Demon class, gargoyles are vicious monster predators. Unlike imps, gargoyles are cunning and ruthless hunters, using their terrifying and nightmarish looks to their advantage.

Ozzie
in the spotlight

Meet the fuzzy star from Avalon—Web of Magic

*H*OT ON THE heels, or paws, of the best-selling book series, "Avalon—Web of Magic," a new star has emerged. The plucky ferret, who is actually an elf stuck in a ferret's body, has found fans all over the world as a starring character in the popular book series. Ozzie recently took a break to answer questions from his fans about what it's like to be a ferret superstar.

Is it fun being in a book series?
Tons. Cousin Schmoot is so proud! He and the other elves are going to be the first in line at the Barns and Acorn in Dingly Dell for the latest release!

How's the adventure going?
It's wild. I never know what's going to happen next. One day I was an elf doing my thing in the Moorgroves and the next, I'm a ferret involved in a great magical quest.

We're helping all the animals that have come to the Ravenswood Preserve and I think it's always a good thing to help animals. Especially now that I know what's it like being fuzzy!

What kind of magic do you have?
Well, none that I know of, but the Fairimentals turned me into a ferret, that's something. Emily thinks there's magic in me that I haven't discovered yet.

Do you think everyone has magic inside of them?
Absolutely. I like the idea of discovering magic inside ourselves. Anyone can feel good about that. Each day if you do something nice for someone else, that's magic because it creates a magical feeling. Calling a friend, or hugging your animal best friend is magical, 'cause it feels good inside.

Do you think you'll ever get back your old body?
One day I think so. But I've got a lot of work to do with

the mages and I realize that the Fairimentals wanted me to have a good disguise. A bear would have been nice. But being a ferret has its advantages.

Like what?
Well, for one, I can climb and run and bake. My paws are very dexterous for using computers and eating.

What's next for Ozzie?
I'm thinking spin-off, "The Amazing Adventures of Ozzie."

When's your birthday?
Why, you got a cake?

What is your real height and weight?
I'm 4 foot 6" 100 pounds

Really? Are you on a diet?
Very funny.

STAR STATS

NAME: Ozymandius

NICKNAME: Ozzie

BIRTHPLACE: Farthingdale

CURRENT RESIDENCE: Ravenswood Preserve,
Stonehill, Pennsylvania

HOBBIES: very good with computers, wigjig dancing

FASCINATING FACT: will eat any kind of cookie;
orders all the supplies for the Pet Palace

Ozzie's Fred-X Home

Dear Mother Elf,

I don't know if you will ever get this letter. We're trying out a new Fred-X transweb delivery service and it's not like I'm in the Moorgroves. In fact, I'm nowhere near home. I'm on a place called Earth. I know you told me not to wander past Dumble Downs, but the Fairimentals called me. That's right, your little elf actually met Fairimentals! You should have seen them: powerful fairies made of earth, air, and water—amazing!

They told me Aldenmor is in danger. Elder Elf Rowthgar was right. There is a poison called Black Fire spreading across our world and it's hurting a lot of creatures. Don't you worry, though—the Fairimentals are protecting

Farthingdale with their magic. They sent me here to find three human mages: a healer, a warrior, and a blazing star. (Check with Auntie Ishris—she knows the stories about humans). Anyway, I found three girls. They hardly know anything about magic so I'm trying to teach them, guide them as best I can. If they can ever work together, they might just learn something. I'll say one thing, they're full of surprises. They've been helping the hurt animals that managed to get here from Aldenmor and I think, given time, they can learn to help the Fairimentals . . . and all of us.

I fear I have a long journey ahead of me before I'll ever see our beautiful elf hills again or enter a prize turnip at the Applecrab Festival. The Fairimentals need to find this place—a place of pure magic, maybe even the source of all magic, Avalon. How can the Fairimentals expect these girls to find such a place? I don't mind telling you I am worried. But if there's anything you taught me, it's that there is nothing you cannot do if you truly believe.

I have no idea where this journey will lead me, but wherever I wander, no matter how far I may be, my heart is with you. Give my regards to Uncle Plith and cousins Schmoot and Tonin. I hope I can make you all proud of me.

Take care and love to all,
Your loving elf,
Ozymandius

P.S. One more thing. Remember you're always saying how you've always wanted a cute, furry pet? Well, if I ever get home, I think you're gonna get one.

Rachel Roberts on Making Magic

*E*MILY, ADRIANE AND KARA started out by helping a handful of animals, then saved the Ravenswood Preserve, and are now on a quest to save the entire Magic Web. Even if you don't have a herd of magical animals or a portal, there's still so much you can do to help. Remembering to turn off lights to save energy, planting a tree, or donating old blankets to an animal shelter are small acts that have a big impact.

My greatest hope for Avalon readers is that these stories will help you discover the magic waiting for you in your own backyard. Once you find it, you'll do everything you can to make it flourish, and your friends will want to get involved, too. One spark of magic can ripple out and make a huge difference, like circles in the stream.

—RACHEL ROBERTS, March, 2008